She was drawn to him...

Dana could feel Alex's energy reach out to her, and the hot African sun grew even hotter under his speculative gaze. Dana had to tilt her head to meet that green gaze of the man half a foot taller than her own five feet eight inches. He wore a faded blue T-shirt that molded the muscles of his arms and chest like a second skin. His cutoffs were frayed, his scandals scuffed, but the casual look didn't hide his animal magnetism.

His full and sensual mouth curved in a half smile. His thick, brown hair grazed the neck of his shirt. Dana registered subliminally that he needed a haircut. What he didn't need was one more ounce of virility. Sensuality simmered in the midday heat.

Dark, handsome, dangerous. Those were the words that came to her mind and wouldn't go away.

ABOUT THE AUTHOR

Shannon Harper and Madeline Porter have been published by Harlequin as Madeline Harper for over ten years. Many of their Temptations have appeared on the Waldenbooks and B. Dalton bestseller lists.

Their partnership is unique since Shannon lives on the East Coast and Madeline on the West, but with the help of faxes, phones and the mail, they have written thirty books, including category romances, time travels, historicals, gothics and mainstream novels. Shannon and Madeline love plotting mysteries and traveling to exotic locales. They were delighted to combine both in their first Intrigue.

Books by Madeline Harper

Tall, Dark and Deadly

Madeline Harper

Harlequin Books

TORONTO • NEW YORK • LONDON
AMSTERDAM • PARIS • SYDNEY • HAMBURG
STOCKHOLM • ATHENS • TOKYO • MILAN
MADRID • WARSAW • BUDAPEST • AUCKLAND

To Bonnie, Debra and Connie, intrepid guides on the journey
into new and unexplored territory.

Porte Ivoire, the Lomawl River and the Bonsuko Swamp are
entirely fictional. However, Pygmy tribes like the Mgembe still
survive in Central Africa and their depiction is based upon first-
person accounts of travelers and explorers. "The Congo" in this
book refers to the People's Republic of Congo. The former
Belgian Congo is now known as Zaire.

ISBN 0-373-22325-0

TALL, DARK AND DEADLY

Copyright © 1995 by Madeline Porter and Shannon Harper

Printed in U.S.A.

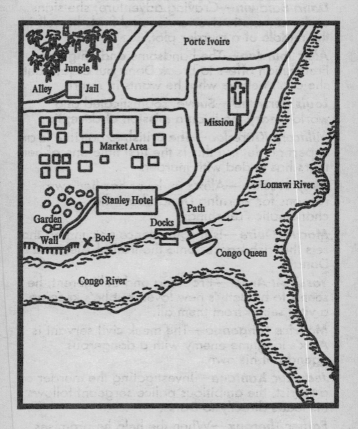

Porte Ivoire

Jungle

Alley   Jail

Mission

Market Area

Lomawi River

Stanley Hotel

Garden   Path

Wall   ✗ Body   Docks

Congo Queen

Congo River

CAST OF CHARACTERS

Dana Baldwin—Craving adventure, she signs up for an exotic river cruise and finds herself in the middle of a murder plot.

Alex Jourdan—The handsome and enigmatic Frenchman offers to break Dana out of jail, but she can't believe what he wants in return.

Louis Bertrand—Suave, sophisticated and world-weary, he is on a mission of deception.

Millicent Kittredge—The British expatriate is an expert guide, but this is the first time one of her tours has ended with murder.

Betty Weston—Alex's ex-lover has her own reasons for warning Dana about the charismatic Frenchman.

Mac McQuire—Is it coincidence or cunning that sets the Irish tracker onto the trail of Alex and Dana?

Yassif Al-Aram—Brooding and belligerent, he seems to be Betty's new lover, but he's keeping a vital secret from them all.

Maurice Longongo—The meek civil servant is Alex's longtime enemy with a dangerous agenda of his own.

Jean-Luc Kantana—Investigating the murder of a tourist, the ambitious police sergeant follows his leads directly to Dana.

Father Theroux—When the help he promises never materializes, Dana knows that even the good priest believes she's guilty.

Prologue

Brazzaville. City of half a million in the African Congo. Its waterfront is always busy; government complexes rise above streets crowded with local markets where merchants will sell anything to the customer willing to pay. Sometimes legally, often not. A melting pot of Congolese, French colonials and expatriates from all over the world, Brazzaville is the place to stake a claim in oil, timber, coffee, diamonds or gold.

An elegant chateau on the edge of the city almost hidden by lush tropical plants that creep around the building, climb its walls and insinuate into its most secret places. Laughter. The pop of corks and flow of wine, the strains of a string quartet. Above it all, in a darkened room, a wooden box lined with purple velvet is opened, revealing its contents. A gloved hand reaches in and removes the prize.

Chapter One

Alex Jourdan leaned back in an old rattan chair on the veranda of his hotel and surveyed the river. The *Congo Queen* was a day late. After five years in Porte Ivoire, Alex wasn't surprised. No doubt the steamer left Brazzaville on schedule, but by the time it hit the far reaches of the Congo River anything could have happened.

He balanced the chair on its two back legs and propped his feet on the porch rail, his routine at this time of day, and one he was getting pretty tired of. He had an ache for something else, something far from Porte Ivoire, far from Brazzaville, and he didn't even know what it was.

"Damn," he swore aloud as he swatted at a mosquito. He was having trouble getting rid of the hotel, but there was another possibility on the horizon. If it worked, he'd be out of here. But would that be enough? The nagging ache persisted, but before he could respond to it, a familiar sound drifted toward him. It was the steamer, downriver, approaching port. The middle of the afternoon was a hell of a time for tourists to arrive, but he wasn't complaining. It meant a night at his hotel for at least a handful of passengers. And if he was any judge, from the sound of the *Congo Queen*'s engine, they might be around for more than one night.

Alex took a long, cold sip of beer and watched the *Congo Queen* limp into port. Same scene, different day. And yet that unexplainable something persisted inside of him.

The old boat docked, and Alex watched as the passengers disembarked. Louis Bertrand was first. Alex meant to watch the Frenchman carefully, but his eyes moved inadvertently to the woman behind him.

Louis stopped, turned and offered his hand to her. Alex's eyes narrowed with interest. Louis always knew how to find a good-looking woman, even on a decrepit old scow like the *Queen* a couple of thousand miles up the Congo.

When Louis stepped aside and the woman disembarked, Alex caught his breath. The Frenchman had found himself one hell of a good-looking female. Blond hair, shining in the sun, pulled back from her face. She was tall and athletic-looking but with rounded breasts and curving hips under her pale violet shirt and beige shorts. And nice long legs. He liked leggy blondes. So he watched her, and he was somehow relieved to see that as soon as Louis helped her off, he moved away. Only polite, not attached, Alex realized.

As she stopped at the wharf to wait for her luggage, Alex tore his eyes away to check out the rest of the guests.

Millicent Kittredge, a frequent visitor at the hotel and leader of innumerable tours of the river, moved along the dock giving orders to the waiting porters. She often recommended tourists to Alex's hotel. For a price. Well, that was okay. Whatever it took.

Millicent was followed by Father Theroux, Porte Ivoire's mission priest. Alex let his eyes drift along the dock until he sighted the blonde again. He got a sensual pleasure from resting his gaze on her cool beauty. The ache inside seemed to dissipate as he drank in her long, lean form.

Reluctantly, he went back to his survey of the other passengers on the debarking plank. Suddenly he sat up straighter and planted his feet on the porch floor. Betty Weston! Now, that was a surprise. He hadn't seen her since . . . well, for a long time. And she wasn't alone. A muscular young man walked down the plank beside her. Alex smiled knowingly. Betty wouldn't be without the companionship of a man for long.

The last passenger off the boat was another familiar face, whom Alex glanced at briefly. Maurice Longongo was a minor government official and major pain in the ass. He was probably checking up again on some imagined violation of an obsolete law that he suspected Alex of breaking at the Stanley Hotel. Frowning, Alex looked at the man again, trying to read his body language. Trouble with the government was to be avoided, especially now.

Alex unwound himself and got up. As he descended the veranda steps and strolled toward the dock to meet the passengers, soon to be guests at his hotel, his pace was leisurely and his demeanor casual. His eyes were on the blonde. She looked hot but not frazzled and perspiring like the others. In fact she seemed to glisten in the midday sun.

Out of the corner of his eye, he saw Millicent bearing down on him like a locomotive. He stepped under the shade of a palm tree and waited. Millicent wore a large straw hat, and her stocky form was encased in what Alex called the Colonial costume, khaki safari jacket and trousers.

He leaned forward as she approached and gave her a kiss, knocking her hat slightly askew. "I see you're still dressing the part, Millie."

"Good for business," she replied in her crisp British tones. "The tourists expect it, but Lord, it's hot! We're going to be with you a little longer than expected," she added. "I'm told that the engine is totally out of commission this time, and the captain has to radio Brazzaville for a part."

Alex grinned. Bad news for the passengers was good news for his pocketbook. Besides, he could use the extra time for his own purposes. Concealing his thoughts, he said, "It amazes me that people still book passage on that old tub."

"Ambience," Millie replied. "Tourists want to experience the real Africa."

The other passengers began to straggle along the path toward the hotel. "Who's the blonde?"

"I thought you'd notice her," Millicent said with a knowing look in her pale blue eyes. "Her name's Dana Baldwin. She's an American. A professor."

He looked past Millicent to the dock. The woman was having trouble with her luggage, and Louis was there to give assistance.

"How did you get away so fast, Millicent? All the other passengers seem to be stuck down there searching for their baggage."

"You haven't noticed in the past, Alex? I have a deal with the captain and his crew. They locate my things for the porters."

"Of course. How stupid of me," he said with a laugh. "I should have known you'd have an angle. Now about the blonde. What's her name...Dana? How'd she get hooked up with your tour?"

"On a whim. She was spending the summer at some kind of language institute in Tangiers. She's fascinated with this region of the Congo and has an obsession with the Pygmies. I told her, of course, that we weren't trekking inland, only doing the river cruise. No Pygmies at all. Just hippos, chimps, the odd leopard on the bank and, of course, my wonderful birds."

"Of course," Alex said, mimicking Millicent's speech. An expatriate British citizen, she'd turned her love of nature into a business and was an avid bird-watcher.

"Dana was determined to come along. Said she had a real need to see the area."

"Hmm." Alex was watching Dana at the wharf and wondering about her.

Millie removed her hat and fanned herself rapidly. "Forget it, Alex. She's just an overzealous language teacher with no hidden agenda."

"Maybe, but you know my philosophy, Millicent. People have only two reasons for traveling to this part of Africa, and that woman is no exception. Either she's running toward something...or away from it."

"You're far too cynical," Millie chastised.

"Porte Ivoire will do that to a person."

"Why don't you get out?"

"You know why, Millie. I can't find a buyer for this damned hotel."

"But you have other irons in the fire, don't you, Alex, other schemes and deals?" Behind thick glasses, her blue eyes were inquisitive.

"Here come the guests," Alex said, ignoring her question. "Time to play the gracious host."

Alex and Millicent watched the commotion at the dock as Father Theroux, surrounded by a phalanx of villagers, turned in the opposite direction, toward his mission, while the others trudged toward the hotel.

Moments later, Betty Weston swept by, eyes cold, head high. "My usual room, Alex?"

"Check with the desk clerk, Betty. You're first in line so you can have any room you want." The muscular young man with her shot Alex a dirty look and followed after Betty.

Millie raised her eyebrows. "Cold shoulder, eh?"

"Icy, I'd say. I wonder why the hell she's here."

"Free-lance journalists are always on the lookout for a story," Millie told him. "I ran into her in Brazzaville. Told her I had some magazine contacts in London eager to buy pieces about wildlife along the river. I assume the boyfriend, Yassif, is for recreational purposes."

"And to put me in my place."

"Did she succeed?" Millicent asked.

Alex laughed. "I'm just relieved that she has someone to occupy her time." He was still watching the wharf. "Wonder what's keeping Louis and the American?"

"Be patient, dear boy." Millicent started to turn toward the hotel, but Alex stopped her. "Stay and introduce me, Millie. And nicely."

"If you insist." Millicent stepped off the path into the shade of the trees. "But let me remind you that it's too late for 'nice.' She's heard all about you. Remember that we've all been together for days on the boat. The talk—"

"Gossip, Millicent."

"Talk, Alex. You can't spend years behaving badly and not expect stories to get around. Your reputation precedes you."

DANA FELT comfortable with Louis. He smelled of French cigarettes and spicy after-shave. A good twenty years older than she but barely taller, he was attractive in a sophisticated, slightly dissipated way—a world-weary man. She'd misplaced a bag; he found it for her. Over her protests, he tipped her porter. Then he took her arm, and they headed up the path toward the hotel. She stopped for a moment, shielded her eyes from the sun's glare and took a long look at the building that was their destination.

"So that's the Stanley Hotel." It was constructed of old brick, faded and mellow, surrounded by a two-story veranda. Charming from the distance, the building looked more and more rickety as they approached. The paint was peeling, the roof sagged and a tangle of vines displaced the mortar between the bricks.

Louis gave a little chuckle. "Not exactly a four-star establishment, eh?"

She was about to respond when someone else did.

"What the hell would *you* know about four-star hotels, Louis?"

A tall man had stepped out of the shadow of the palm trees and blocked their path. Millicent was standing beside him, but Dana scarcely noticed. She was lost in the greenest eyes she'd ever seen, cool eyes that met hers with a look of long and thorough appraisal. Dana tried to look away, but it wasn't possible. Her eyes were locked on his.

She heard Millicent's voice. "Dana, this is Alex Jourdan. Our host. Alex, meet Dana Baldwin, one of our tour members not yet initiated into the ways of Porte Ivoire.'' Millicent gave an amused little twist to her smile.

Dana could feel Alex's energy reach out to her, and the sultry African sun grew even hotter under his speculative gaze. Dana had to tilt her head to meet Alex's green eyes; he had to be half a foot taller than her own five feet eight inches. He wore a faded blue T-shirt that molded the muscles of his arms and chest like a second skin. His cutoffs were frayed, his sandals scuffed, but the casual look didn't hide his animal magnetism.

His full and sensual mouth curved in a half smile. His thick, dark brown hair grazed the neck of his shirt. Dana registered subliminally that he needed a haircut. What he didn't need was one more ounce of virility. Sensuality simmered in the midday heat.

Dark, handsome, dangerous. Those were the words that came to her mind and wouldn't go away.

''*Bienvenu.* Welcome to Porte Ivoire and to the Stanley Hotel,'' he said at last in a voice that was deep and husky with a trace of French accent. Only a hint, enough to make it both memorable and sexy as hell. She'd heard a great deal on the boat about women who'd fallen under Alex Jourdan's spell. Now she understood.

''I hope you enjoy your stay,'' he added when she didn't reply.

Everyone seemed to be waiting for a response. Dana finally managed to include the hotel in her gaze while not quite tearing it away from Alex. ''Thank you. I'm sure I'll enjoy every moment.'' God, she thought, *every moment!* Why did she say that?

''The moments could turn to days,'' Millicent reminded her. ''If that engine doesn't get repaired.''

Alex didn't seem to be listening. "How do you like my hotel?"

"It's very—interesting," Dana managed to say.

Alex laughed, a deep, rich sound. "I think of the old building as a grand lady past her prime, a little tawdry but with quite a past. A lady with many secrets." His smile intimated that he might be willing to share those secrets with Dana. "Let me take that for you." He reached for the bag she had slung over her shoulder.

"That's all right, I—"

It was too late. His hand was on her arm, insinuating upward and under the strap of the bag, which he slipped off her shoulder. "I'll get you checked in."

Louis spoke up. "Ignoring your old *ami*, eh, Alex? Well, in the company of one so lovely, that is understandable."

Dana saw Alex's eyes flicker quickly to Louis and then back to her. "I didn't expect you to turn up, Bertrand," he said coolly.

"But you know how much I love the river, and I needed a respite from the heat and crowds of Brazzaville. I had delightful company aboard the steamer. As for this young lady, you will be interested, as I certainly was, to learn that she shares my fascination with the Mgembe. The Pygmies, you know."

Alex gave Louis a long look and shrugged. "To each his own, Bertrand. And now, ladies..." He bowed slightly. "If you'll come into the lobby with me. Oh, and you, too, Bertrand," he added as an afterthought.

"You have one more guest," Louis reminded him. "Monsieur Longongo is still loading down the porters with his bags. He cannot manage to travel light."

Alex glanced at the little man just leaving the dock. "Maybe by the time he gets here, all my rooms will be booked." With that, he slung Dana's bag over his shoulder and led the way into the hotel.

DANA opened the door, stepped into her room and into a scene out of an old movie. Crossing on mahogany plank floors, she dropped her bag onto a simple iron bedstead painted white with a bright colored spread. Overhead a slow-moving ceiling fan circulated the humid air.

Admittedly, the flowered wallpaper was peeling a little, the throw rugs faded, the bedspread worn. But that was part of the charm. As Alex had said, the hotel was a little past its prime but still grand.

She closed the door, almost expecting a director to shout, "Cut." A slight smile spread over her face. If she was acting out a role in an old movie, she was also thinking about the film's hero, a handsome hotelier with a wicked reputation. She crossed the room and pushed open the French doors to the upper-level veranda. The Congo River lay before her, curving like a huge serpent, slithering into the depths of the tropical rain forest.

Her own private movie was interrupted when Betty Weston stepped onto the veranda next door. "At least the hotel has a nice view," the redhead said grudgingly.

"All this is new to me," Dana admitted, "and very exciting."

Betty faced her, leaning back against the railing. "Yes, you are rather a novice." Her brown eyes were hard and glittering. "I saw you with him."

"Him?"

"Alex, of course. I thought you'd heard enough about him on the boat."

"I try not to listen to gossip," Dana responded.

Betty snorted with disgust. "You won't have to worry about gossip if we're here long enough. You'll find out for yourself what a cold and ruthless man he is—"

Dana was speechless at the angry words.

"Oh, he's interested in you," Betty went on. "He always likes new women, but in the long run, he's after one of two things. Sex or money. So remember to lock your door—and hide your valuables."

The knock on Dana's door was a welcome sound. Without hesitation, she made her apologies to Betty and left the veranda. Millicent was waiting at her door.

"Oh, there you are, dear. I've come to take you shopping."

"But we just got here, Millicent. I haven't even unpacked or had a chance to rest—"

"Rest, on your first day in Porte Ivoire? Ridiculous! You have to see the native quarter and go to the market. They're just opening up again after the midday break. You won't believe the beautiful fabrics. I know a little shop—"

Dana started to respond, but Millicent was on a roll. "Rest!" she repeated. "I'm sixty-three. Did you know that? And I can go all day. How old are you?"

"Twenty-six," Dana responded.

"Then you can probably keep up with me."

"You bet I can," Dana promised. "Let's go shopping."

DANA WISHED she could take back those words a dozen times during their shopping trip. Most of the villagers and half the inhabitants of the surrounding countryside seemed to be crowded into the Port Ivoire bazaar.

Shoppers called back and forth and children chased one another among the thatched-roof shops that sold everything from live chickens to intricately carved figurines. The scents of cooking meat and stewing spices wafted on the air, mingled with the cacophony of half a dozen different dialects. The market was loud and frenetic, hot and dusty. And overhead the relentless sun beat down.

The heat wasn't all that got to Dana; so did Millicent's relentless advice and cheerful instructions.

"No, no, dear. Not that pottery. You can buy it much more cheaply at another shop," she whispered, drawing Dana away from a display of brightly painted pots. "Besides, this is not nearly as special as the carvings. And of course the cloth. And, oh, I know a wonderful shop where you can buy jewelry, authentic pieces, hand set—"

Dana asserted herself. "I'm not buying, I'm just looking, Millie. And I'm sure I'll get around to all the shops eventually."

Millicent sighed. "Of course. I forget what it's like to come here for the first time. But when it's time to buy, let me be your adviser, dear, so you won't be taken advantage of." She wagged a warning finger.

"Thanks, Millie. I will." Dana stepped out of the sun into the doorway of a corner shop, hoping for a hint of breeze. There was none. She mopped at the dampness on her forehead with a tissue. "I'm a little overwhelmed by all this activity—and heat," Dana admitted. "But I don't want to hold you back, Millie."

"Well…" Millie adjusted her hat to better shade her face. "I am anxious to visit a friend at the other side of the bazaar. She sells the most fabulous handwoven rugs. I'm taking a few back to Brazzaville on consignment. You'd love—"

Dana laughed at Millie's energy and enthusiasm. "I'm sure I would, but I'm not going to carry rugs back on the plane. Go ahead, see your friend. I'll wander around on this side of the market. It's a little shadier," she added.

"Are you sure, dear?" Millie asked solicitously.

"I'm sure. I'll look around for a little while and then go back to the hotel." Dana could tell she was cramping Millie's energetic style. "Go on. It's okay."

"Such a dear girl," Millie said. "Now be careful what you eat around here or you might end up with toasted grub worms." Millie chuckled at her humor.

"I'm going to browse, not eat," Dana called after her. "And I'm not buying anything."

BACK AT THE HOTEL, Dana looked at her purchases. Why, when she'd only meant to browse, had she invested in yards of bright colored cloth, a carved leopard and a huge straw hat? She'd have plenty of time later to explore the markets at her leisure, maybe find some real bargains on items she actually wanted. Oh, well, she decided, her purchases were interesting.

She tossed everything on a chair, kicked off her shoes and flopped onto her bed. As the fan whirred hypnotically, the sounds of the river seemed to recede and float away on the hot, moist air. Dana closed her eyes.

She forgot about Millicent, her shopping trip, the useless purchases...and she thought about Alex. She didn't mean to, but she couldn't stop herself. Behind closed eyes, she envisioned his face, imagined his voice, even felt his touch on her shoulder.

Betty was right. She'd heard about him on the boat coming upriver—and she *had* listened to the gossip; there was no denying that. Louis had told her about himself and Alex, that they'd been great friends until they'd argued violently over a woman. Louis also hinted that Millicent and Alex had some sort of deal going; he paid her a percentage for each guest she steered to his hotel. Even with engine trouble, the *Congo Queen*'s captain somehow managed to make it as far as the Stanley Hotel.

What had Millicent said about Alex? As Dana tried to remember, his face drifted in and out of her mind's eye again. She tried to hold onto Millicent's words, but his face kept smiling down at her suggestively.

Then she remembered. Millicent's accusations involved smuggling. Diamonds? Gold? She wasn't sure. But there was no doubt that Alex Jourdan had a reputation for walking a little outside the law.

And what about Betty? Dana thought of her bizarre encounter with the journalist. Never had she seen a woman so bitter over a failed affair, and everyone on the boat seemed to be sure there'd been one between Alex and Betty. More gossip, which Dana had tried unsuccessfully to avoid.

Now she put it out of her mind but couldn't dismiss *him* so easily. Even as she felt herself drifting away on a soft wave of sleep, his face was still there. Then through the haze of drowsiness, she heard his voice again, but this time he was talking to someone. It sounded like Louis. They were arguing. Outside? On the veranda? In the hallway?

The voices seemed real, not imaginary, not dreamlike. They were raised in anger. She tried to concentrate on their words. She caught one. Pygmy. Something about the Pygmies... Everything went fuzzy in her mind, but Dana hung on, listening. They were arguing about—what? An elephant or elephants? Then she heard her name. Or thought she did.

Dana tried to hold onto consciousness, but she kept falling, falling. And then she slept.

SHE MADE IT to dinner that night with the conversation still ringing in her ears. And when she observed the two men seated at opposite ends of a long table, not speaking, their eyes rarely meeting, Dana decided the conversation hadn't been a dream. But she chose to sit at their table anyway, rather than join Betty and Yassif or Mr. Longongo, who dined alone, or the captain and his crew, who shared another table.

Dana sat down beside Father Theroux. Apparently, he often dined at the hotel. Tonight he joined Millicent in trying to keep up a lively conversation while Alex and Louis silently glowered. As for Dana, she had her own agenda. Pygmies. And elephants. That's what Alex and Louis had been arguing about, and she was determined to get it out in the open. Curiosity guiding her, Dana directed her questions to the priest, a willing participant.

Louis seemed disinterested, more concerned about his bottle of wine than conversation, while Alex lounged back in his chair and observed the room. He'd obviously just bathed. His skin gleamed, and drops of water still sparkled in his hair. He'd changed into a clean, crisp white shirt of gauzy material that draped across the muscles of his shoulders and chest. His rolled-up sleeves revealed the strength of his lower arms, and the white shirt set off his tan and green eyes. Dana had to force her attention away from Alex's physical attributes and back to the priest.

"Yes, it is true that I have lived all my life in the Congo," Theroux said in answer to a question, "but I have seen the Pygmy only a few times. And never has one member of the Mgembe tribe been converted to Catholicism." His dark eyes glowed sadly. "It would gladden my heart if such would happen, but—" He shrugged his thin shoulders.

"Maybe someday," Dana said.

Millicent spoke up. "I'm appalled that the Mgembe still hunt elephant, which is an endangered species. Everyone knows that."

Conveniently, Millicent had switched from Pygmies to elephants, almost as if she'd been guided by Dana. "Is that true?" Dana asked. "Do they still hunt?"

"Elephants are protected," the priest said, "but the Pygmies obey no rules except their own. Who knows what they do, hidden away in the rain forest."

Alex suddenly leaned forward, his gaze on Dana. For an instant she thought there was suspicion in his eyes. Or was it just curiosity, like her own? "Why are you so interested in the Pygmies?" he asked. "Most of the world has never heard of the Mgembe."

"I inherited my interest from my father, Phillip Baldwin. He was in the Congo years ago and began a study that I would like to complete. If only I could get to the Pygmies..."

"Not much chance of that," Alex said dismissively. But if he paid little attention to her goals, he paid plenty to *her*, surveying her with his potent gaze.

"It's true that not many people know about the Mgembe," Dana agreed. "Except for Monsieur Bertrand." She smiled at Louis, who was pouring himself another glass of wine.

"Louis is a wonder, isn't he?" Alex commented. "So eager to share his knowledge, especially if the questioner is young and pretty."

Dana felt herself flush, and to cover, she turned on Alex. "Louis was only being polite by answering my questions."

Millicent, who'd watched the byplay speculatively, directed her remark to Alex. "You and Louis used to be such good friends, I hate to see you on the outs."

Louis rose from his chair. "Alex is not an easy man for one to remain friends with, madame. If you will excuse me..." Wineglass in hand, he headed for the veranda.

"I'll see after him," Father Theroux offered.

"Coffee?" Alex asked the women without skipping a beat, as if nothing had happened. "Perhaps in the garden..."

Millicent spoke for both of them. "That would be delightful. And a little cognac, too, Alex, dear."

But Millicent didn't make it to the garden. Mr. Longongo cornered her, and as Dana passed by his table, she heard a snatch of his long, involved questions about a partial refund of his tour fee since the boat had broken down. He reminded Dana of a ferret with sharp little features and darting black eyes. There was something creepy about the man, she decided as she drifted into the garden alone.

The air was sweet with the fragrance of jungle flowers and, as always, the dark mysterious scent of the mighty Congo. Dana wrapped her arms around herself and took a deep breath, throwing back her head, breathing the rich, heady scent of the jungle air. The moon rode low in the sky, huge, round, so close she felt she could touch it. Despite the delays and problems, the petty arguments of the others, she felt wonderful.

She was in Africa! A stone's throw from the Congo, and even if she never saw her first Pygmy, this was already the adventure of her life. She closed her eyes and inhaled pure excitement.

She didn't hear the footsteps approaching on the sandy path, and when a hand touched her shoulder, Dana jumped, startled. "Don't be afraid," a voice told her, in a tone so soft and low that it heightened her fear rather than dispelling it. She started to move away, toward the hotel, and then she recognized him.

The vague shadowy figure in the moonlight was Alex. "I decided to skip the coffee," he told her. "My cognac is excellent. French. A hundred years old and saved for special guests." He handed her a glass.

"Thanks." For an instant his long fingers curled around hers. He was so near that she could smell the scent of his tangy after-shave and hear the even flow of his breathing. There was something dark and compelling about him that made her nervous even as it attracted her. She didn't know how to behave around him, and she certainly had no idea what he would do next.

She took a step away from him and raised the glass to her lips. A warm glow began in the pit of her stomach and spread upward, but she couldn't relax. Not when Alex was still too damn close to her, not when her heart refused to slow down.

She wanted him to move away. The blatant sexuality that emanated from him made her uncomfortable. He seemed so damned sure of himself, as if she was his for the asking, as if she'd arranged a romantic rendezvous in the garden especially for him. To cover her nervousness, she took another sip from her glass.

"Like it?" His voice was as smooth and rich as the cognac, and she was afraid that it could have the same power over her.

"Yes, it's wonderful. But now—" She handed Alex the glass and attempted to step around him.

Holding her with his his eyes, he let both glasses slip from his grasp and drop onto the sandy path. She looked down at them, startled. Then he encircled her waist with his hands and pulled her close. "You're not running away from me, are you, Dana?" The strength that she'd feared in his voice had become a power of intimacy—and danger.

"No, of course not," she lied. "I just want to get away from, I mean get out of, the night air. It's..." Her voice trailed off and she realized she didn't want to get away at all, not when she saw Alex so clearly in the moonlight, his lips parted in a smile to reveal even white teeth that gleamed against his tanned skin. Hungry light glowed deep in his green eyes. Dana shivered, and she didn't know why. Was it excitement—or fear?

He still held her, easily now, with one hand lingering on her waist, the other at the small of her back. The warmth from his body reached out and caressed her. She felt an urge to touch his face, run her fingers across his cheek and chin. But she willed her hands to stay at her sides. Alex Jourdan was trouble.

He looked at her with a knowing, intimate smile as if he'd read her thoughts. "I've been waiting for you, Dana." His breath was warm against her face.

"What do you mean by waiting?" Her voice sounded breathy, surprised, not like her at all. And her heart— why couldn't she control its erratic pounding?

"Waiting for a long-legged blonde to come into my life. Now you're here, and I'm glad."

He slid his hand from her waist upward along her back, beneath the fabric of her blouse. His touch was sensual, practiced, erotic. And her skin tingled wherever he touched her.

Alarm bells went off inside Dana's head even while her body responded. Alex Jourdan was handsome and exciting, and there was a part of her that wanted to know him, that desired to be swept away by his dark, romantic power.

But the other side of her was more careful, even wary. He was a man with a disreputable past, a womanizer and, according to the gossip, a probable cheat if not a possible crook. He was certainly a stranger, not someone to be alone with in the dark night.

Dana struggled to get her voice under control. "I didn't come here for a romantic fling." Even as she made the statement, she realized how uptight and foolish she sounded.

To make her seem even more ridiculous, he repeated the words. "A romantic fling?" His voice was amused. "I never suggested that, Professor. But since you mention it, just why did you come to Porte Ivoire?"

To find you. The thought blazed across her mind even while she fought to keep from saying it aloud. The intensity of it frightened her. And when his eyes met hers in a long look, she was held by what she saw there. Recognition. Acceptance. Desire. For an instant in the moonlight his face was serious, almost brooding, and she was overcome again by an irresistible urge to touch his face, draw his mouth down on hers.

Instead, she took a deep breath and shoved against his chest with both hands. "Let me go, Alex. If you don't I'll—"

"You'll what?" he teased. "You don't seem like a violent woman."

"I'm not," she snapped. "But I might become one. Now let me go."

He took one step backward, shoved his hands into his pockets and gazed at her, a sardonic smile playing around his lips. He appeared more amused than perturbed by her reaction. "You have even more fire than I imagined, Dana Baldwin. I like that. Cool on the outside, hot and—"

Dana turned and walked away with his words echoing in her head. Her legs were shaky, and her hands were damp with perspiration. Dammit, she was doing just what he'd said. She was running. Fleeing from him and herself. She was confused by her reaction to Alex and the emotions he unleashed. She hadn't handled the situation well at all, and she vowed to be more in charge next time they met. Or to stay away from him. That was the best way, she decided as she hurried up the steps, across the veranda—and straight into Louis Bertrand.

Chapter Two

"*Chérie*, slow down. You will hurt yourself."

"Sorry," she mumbled, drawing in the night air in huge gulps. "I'm a little . . ." She struggled for words.

"*Agitée?*" He looked over her shoulder toward the shadowy form in the garden. "Alex. I should have known. You must forgive him. He does not stop to think. For Alex, to make love is as natural as to breathe."

"Make love? No, he just made a pass, he didn't—"

Louis chuckled softly. "In French 'make love' can be no more than to touch or even suggest. It is all love-making in our language. And when a beautiful woman appears . . ."

"I think there's a compliment there somewhere," she managed, "but he's so damned arrogant—"

"On this we agree." Louis took her arm. "Shall we walk by the river and cool off? There's a delightful breeze, and I assure you I'm quite sober now. And unlike my rude friend, I shall make no passes."

Dana hesitated, but Louis held her firmly by the elbow and kept the conversation going. "You see, the problem with Alex is that he is only one half French. His mother was American, and he spent many years in the States. This is not to say anything negative about your country," he added graciously, "but over there he lost something of the French savoir faire women so much admire."

"He's lacking something. You're right about that," Dana muttered. "Manners, to begin with."

"Indeed," Louis replied. "He does not have an abundance of manners. Also, he can be quite ruthless when he has to be. But enough talk of Alex. He is only an innkeeper in an outpost far from civilization. Instead, let us speak of the Pygmies, which we both find so fascinating."

"I thought perhaps you had lost interest in the subject."

"And why is that, my dear?"

"Well, at dinner—"

"Oh, yes. I avoided conversation," he admitted.

"So did Alex."

"Hmm." Louis stopped. "May I smoke?"

"Of course."

He lit a narrow black cigarillo and inhaled deeply. "We both avoided conversation at the table tonight, Alex and I," Louis said. "The reasons for this are very complicated."

Dana waited, wondering if he would mention the other conversation, the one she'd heard—or thought she'd heard—as she dozed off in her room.

"But I will not bother you with this," he said.

"Please, it's all right."

"No, no," he insisted. "There are more important subjects for us to talk about."

Before she could respond, they were interrupted by the approach of another couple coming toward them along the path. Betty and Yassif.

They stepped aside. "Lovely evening, is it not?" Louis asked pleasantly.

Betty nodded, but Yassif only scowled.

"Pleasant fellow," Louis joked when they were out of earshot.

"I wonder what she sees in him," Dana began before realizing the naïveté of the question.

They stopped at a crumbling wall near the riverbank. Thick green vegetation crept toward them, seemingly overwhelming everything in its path. A hazy mist enveloped the night and magnified the great silence that surrounded them. It was both fascinating and eerie.

"About the Pygmies. You wish to travel even farther into the mysterious jungle in search of them," Louis said.

"Yes, I do. Now I have the perfect opportunity, since we're going to be stuck here for a while. I realize you're reluctant to take me to them, but maybe there's someone you could recommend."

"There are no guides in this village, but perhaps some miles upstream." Louis puffed silently and stared out into the blackness. "A man named McQuire once took me deep into the rain forest."

"McQuire," Dana repeated. "An Englishman?"

"Irishman, I believe. He has been a guide for over thirty years. Of course, I don't know if he is still alive." Louis shrugged elegantly. "As I have told you, the jungle is a dangerous place."

"I understand that," Dana said impatiently, "but maybe I could see the fringes, at least. What's the point of being in the Congo if I can't have an adventure or two?"

Louis looked amused "Indeed, what is the point of life...without an adventure or two? And nowhere is there more possibility for excitement than here on the banks of the Congo. A thousand miles of brown ribbon cutting through a carpet of green, and on the river time means nothing. We live for the day."

"How romantic," Dana said.

"When a Frenchman speaks of the Congo, it is always romantic," Louis replied with a smile.

"There's just one problem."

"And what is that, dear Dana?"

"The mosquitoes!" They were buzzing around her head. She slapped at them ineffectually. "They're driving me crazy. I'm afraid I'll have to go inside."

"I understand, although they seem to avoid me," Louis said with a soft laugh. "Perhaps it is the smoke from my cigarillo. Meanwhile, remember your anti-malaria pills, a must here in Africa."

"I will, but for now—"

"Yes, go to your mosquito netting," Louis said, "and as for me, I shall stay here a while longer and smoke."

"Then good night," Dana said. "I'll see you in the morning. Maybe we can find that McQuire fellow."

"Maybe," Louis said softly. *"Au revoir, chérie."*

He watched her walk away, enjoying the soft flow of her dress as it caressed her hips and the bounce of her hair on her shoulders. He'd found Dana lovely from the first moment, and it was no wonder that Alex felt the same. Alex, Louis thought, so precipitative and aggressive. Not the kind of man to let well enough alone.

Louis took a last drag on his cigarillo and drew the thick, pungent smoke deep into his lungs. Was there anything more pleasant, he wondered, than standing near the world's most magnificent river, replete with good food and wine, as he watched the delicate movement of a beautiful woman walking through the night?

If there was, Louis couldn't imagine.

He sighed deeply, turned toward the river and never noticed the barely perceptible movement of the high grass on the hillside. Nor did he hear the soft, deadly sound that followed. He only felt the sting, like that of a night insect, in the soft tissue of his neck. The pain came an instant later, causing him to grasp his throat with both hands, as he choked for breath.

Suddenly he knew—he understood! But it was too late. Louis sank to his knees, fell forward, hitting his head on the stone wall, and then crumpled to the ground and lay still.

"THIS IS NOT a good way to begin a day. Not good at all," Police Sergeant Jean Luc Kantana confided dourly to Alex. "To be awakened at three in the morning to the news that crew members returning to the *Congo Queen* stumbled over a dead body. And then to discover it is the body of Louis Bertrand—"

Alex stared straight ahead, his face set like granite. His thoughts were dark, as they had been since the moment news had come to him that Louis's body had been found. But he wasn't about to console Kantana. The policeman wasn't his problem.

"I'm not pleased myself to learn that my old friend is dead and the Stanley has been taken over by gendarmes."

"All proper protocol will be observed, my friend," Kantana assured. "We will, of course, question Porte Ivoire locals, but my instincts tell me..." The sergeant's words faded as he looked around the hotel lobby where Alex had gathered the guests.

"You think the killer is in this group?" Alex regarded Kantana curiously. "Why would you suspect that?" He'd known Kantana for five years and hoped he could use that friendship to find out what was on the policeman's mind.

Kantana answered obliquely. "Most murders in Porte Ivoire are easily solved. Two men fight in a bar over a woman. A woman knifes her philandering husband. This, I believe, is different from the usual local crime."

"Louis was killed with a dart from a blowgun, Jean Luc. I would suggest that's a local weapon."

"Such paraphernalia can be purchased up and down the Congo by any of your guests. Or by you." His smile was cool. "Everyone is a suspect, Alex. The death of a foreigner must be carefully investigated. And now, I must get to work."

He stepped away from Alex and addressed the room. "*Mesdames* and *messieurs*. It is time to begin. Mademoiselle Baldwin, shall we start with you?"

Dana had struggled to control her shock, but her hands shook noticeably as she raised her coffee cup to her lips. "I was with him by the river," she said softly, almost to herself. "We were talking, making plans—"

She broke off, aware of everyone's eyes on her. Kantana's were alert and probing, but his dark, handsome face revealed nothing.

"Plans?" His voice was deceptively soft and gentle.

Dana attempted to explain. "Tentative plans to find a guide to take me into Pygmy territory. We talked about going together. Maybe..." Her voice trailed off.

"I see." Kantana nodded solemnly. "You have knowledge of the Mgembe?"

The room was still, the only sound a gentle whirring of the overhead fan. Alex leaned against the arched doorway of the lobby, his lanky body perfectly relaxed, one hand in his pocket. He'd passed up coffee and was sipping a cognac and watching Kantana, not Dana. Everyone else's eyes seemed to be focused on her.

On a rattan love seat beside the door, Betty and Yassif sat side by side, staring at her, Betty's face sharp and unfriendly, Yassif's sleepy-eyed and sullen. Huddled quietly in a corner, Maurice Longongo watched her with his ferret eyes. Dana felt herself shiver involuntarily. Even Millicent, who had stopped her bustle to refill coffee cups, watched and waited.

"The Mgembe?" Kantana repeated.

"I was interested in them. Everyone knew that." Her gaze took in the whole room. "But Louis seemed to be the most knowledgeable, and certainly he was the most helpful."

Kantana scribbled on a pad. "Now Mademoiselle Baldwin, tell me please, at what time did you walk with Monsieur Bertrand by the river?"

"After dinner. I'm not sure."

"Immediately after dinner?" Kantana pressed.

"No, I—" Dana hesitated, wondering whether or not to mention her encounter with Alex in the garden. She glanced quickly at him, but his eyes were still on the policeman.

"About ten o'clock," Betty said with authority. "Yassif and I were returning to the hotel and saw them heading toward the river. I guess we're witnesses."

Dana shot her a surprised look. *Witnesses?*

Kantana made a careful note. "And how long did you remain with him?"

"Not long. The mosquitoes drove me away." Dana remembered her farewell to Louis, the sound of his soft *au revoir* floating on the hot night air, and her eyes filled with tears. "Maybe if I'd stayed with him, this wouldn't have happened."

Millicent crossed to Dana's chair and patted her on the shoulder. "There, there, dear. No one blames you for what happened to poor Louis."

Maybe not, but Dana felt as if all of them, even Millicent, were skeptical. "He was your friend, too, Millicent."

"Yes, he was, for many years," she replied.

"I'm so sorry," Dana offered.

"It's not your fault."

There it was again, the release from blame that was somehow damning.

"Why would anyone want to kill Louis?" Dana asked. "He was so sweet and gentle."

"That's not exactly true," Betty snapped. "He was also involved in all sorts of sordid little deals. Louis was no angel despite the fact that he stuck like a leech to Father Theroux on the trip."

That was true, Dana remembered. He'd seemed devoted to the elderly man. The wine merchant and the village priest—an unlikely pairing.

"Dear Lord, one of us needs to tell Father Theroux about Louis," Millicent said.

"I'm sure he knows," Alex replied laconically. "News travels fast in Porte Ivoire. Especially bad news."

"The priest will be told—and questioned," Kantana said coolly, dismissing the subject and moving on to continue his interrogation of Dana. "Did anyone notice you returning to the hotel?"

"I don't think so." She looked around the room hopefully, but no one spoke up. "I used the side steps to the second-floor veranda. Then I went directly to my room and to bed."

Kantana wrote on his pad and then one by one asked each of the other guests their whereabouts from ten o'clock until the body was found. He listened carefully to the responses.

"So," he said as he completed the rounds, "each of you was alone in your bedroom—"

"Yassif and I were together," Betty announced, reaching for her lover's hand. "Some of us have nothing to worry about. *We* have alibis."

"Some of us have been known to lie." That was Alex. His remark caused Betty's face to redden. She opened her mouth to reply and then thought better of it.

Kantana continued without missing a beat. "With the exception of Mademoiselle Weston and Monsieur Al-Aram, who were together—so they say—and my friend Alex, who was in his office."

"I often stay up late," came Alex's response.

Kantana got to his feet. "Now I must ask your further indulgence. At this time we will search your rooms."

Millicent reacted immediately. "Search our rooms? Surely, you joke, Sergeant. Why in the world? The man was killed with a *blow dart*. Obviously by someone right here in Porte Ivoire—"

Kantana's reply was as smooth as silk. "So it would seem, as you say, considering the murder weapon. But we have reasons to look elsewhere."

"Why?" Millicent shot back.

"We found a passport and a wallet filled with cash on the body. What does that mean to you?" he asked the room in general.

Longongo responded, speaking for the first time that morning in his high nasal voice with his impeccable clipped syllables. "It negates the prime motive, perhaps the only one, for murder by a local person, namely robbery. Which means one of us must have another motive. What would that be?"

"I do not know yet," Kantana admitted, "but I expect to uncover the motive along with the means and the opportunity. And when all three come together, I shall have my killer."

He snapped his notebook shut, and Dana shivered again. She'd pulled on shorts and a T-shirt when the clerk awakened her. Now, in the cool of dawn, she needed something warmer.

"If I could go to my room for a moment first—" she said to Kantana.

"No, mademoiselle. That would defeat our purpose."

"I don't understand. I just need to get something warm to put on—"

"Nothing will be removed until after our search." His voice had a sharp edge.

Once again, she was made to feel guilty. And just because she was cold.

"Each of you will remain here until the search is completed." With a slight bow, he turned and went out, followed by his aide.

THE MORNING seemed interminable. The hotel cooks prepared and set out breakfast, but no one seemed to have much of an appetite. Dana picked at a bowl of fruit, and everyone else did, too. Most of them drank innumerable cups of coffee, including Alex, who had switched from cognac.

When Kantana came downstairs from his search of the guests' rooms, he commandeered Alex's office to interview the guests—or suspects, as Dana had begun to think of herself and the others. She tried to give the word a sardonic twist in her mind because it was ridiculous, of course, to think any of them might have murdered Louis Bertrand, but she was still nervous.

Someone *had* murdered him, and Kantana seemed convinced that it wasn't a citizen of Porte Ivoire but one of the guests in the Stanley Hotel, or Alex himself, or even Father Theroux.

Slowly they went into the office one by one. First Longongo and then Millicent completed their interviews and returned to their rooms. Yassif was next.

Dana waited silently while Alex disappeared into the kitchen, apparently to communicate with his staff, and Betty paced nervously up and down, glancing at the closed door.

"Don't worry," Dana assured her, "Yassif is a big boy. He can answer his own questions."

Betty puffed out her cheeks and then fell down onto the love seat. "It's just that he doesn't speak English very well. His French is worse."

"Kantana is very patient," Dana said, wondering suddenly why she should be attempting to pacify Betty, of all people.

"I'm also concerned because our relationship is so new. I'm a little overprotective of Yassif."

Dana couldn't find anything encouraging to say about that. She really didn't want to talk about Betty's romance with the surly Yassif.

But Betty did. "We met at a party in Brazzaville just before the trip upriver."

"Did Millicent introduce you?" Dana *was* curious about that.

Betty bristled. "Yassif and Millicent? Of course not, he'd never be seen with someone like her."

"I saw them together on the *Congo Queen,* several times." A little perverse of her to mention that, Dana realized, but she couldn't resist.

"And I saw you talk with Louis. Yet you and he weren't friends, or so you say." Betty raised her eyebrows meaningfully.

"Give it a rest, Betty." That was Alex, appearing at the doorway. "You're not going to get a story out of this."

"That's what you're after?" Dana asked, confronting Betty. "You want to write about Louis's death!"

She shrugged. "Why not? A good juicy murder is certainly more interesting than a piece about wildlife of the Congo."

Dana couldn't control her disgust. Betty was thinking about this whole horrible episode as a magazine story and had no feelings at all for poor Louis, dead less than twelve hours. Dana mentally took off the gloves. Betty wasn't going to get any sympathy from her.

Apparently, no one would get sympathy from Alex, who leaned against the lobby doorway, his face unreadable. Dana avoided his eyes, but Betty glared angrily at him. Then she was called by Kantana, and Dana was left alone with Alex.

She felt awkward and uncomfortable around him, with the remembrance of their scene in the garden fresh in her mind. But there was something else going on that she couldn't put her finger on. He seemed to be studying her intently, as if he was sizing her up. Could he possibly think she was involved in Louis's death?

Deciding that the best defense was a strong offense, she asked, "Did you go directly to your office last night after you left me in the garden?"

"Playing detective, Dana?"

"I've been wondering about that," she replied. Which was true. She was curious about Alex and where he'd been while she and Louis were by the river. He easily could have followed them.

Alex strolled to the buffet table and poured a cup of coffee. "I'll answer your question because I have nothing to hide—unlike some of the guests." His smile was ingenuous. "After our rendezvous in the garden where you obviously misunderstood my overtures of friendship—"

Dana gritted her teeth at his cynical misrepresentation of the episode.

"—I went to my office, spurned and saddened, to bury myself in work." His eyes sparkled with humor as he watched her surprised reaction. "Good story, isn't it? In fact, I don't have an alibi, but neither do you. And you were the last to see Louis alive," he added softly.

Dana quickly defended herself. "But you were the one who argued with him."

Before Alex could respond, the office door opened and Betty emerged. The supercilious look on the redhead's face caused Dana's heart to sink; it was a look that bore her no goodwill.

An aide ushered Dana into Alex's office to face the sergeant. Her knees were shaky, and her heart was pounding like a drum. For no reason! She had nothing to be afraid of.

Kantana sat behind Alex's desk looking solemn and official. The tall, sullen-looking officer dressed in khaki stood behind Kantana staring straight ahead. The sergeant gestured to a straight-backed chair. Dana sank onto it, wiping her damp palms against her shorts. What more could he ask her? What more could she tell him? The silence became ominous and oppressive. And when Kantana finally spoke to her, she jumped at the sound of his voice.

"Do you know what this is, mademoiselle?"

Dana leaned forward to look at what he held in his hand. She recognized it immediately, a long wooden tube, intricately carved. She recalled pictures in her father's notes, descriptions of an ancient weapon still used by the Pygmies. What Kantana held in his hand was a blowgun.

"I know what it is, but I've never seen that one before."

"Ah, yes." Kantana put down the weapon and carefully touched his fingertips together, forming a kind of tent with his elegant hands. He leaned back in his chair and spoke in a low voice. "Then how, mademoiselle, do you explain its presence in your room?"

Dana couldn't believe the question. "You couldn't have found that in my room. I've never seen it in my life!"

"But it *was* found in your room, mademoiselle."

"No. There's been a mistake. That isn't mine. Someone else left it in the room, maybe a previous guest—"

"No," the sergeant said crisply. "I have interviewed the maid on your floor. She cleaned the room thoroughly before you moved in. There was nothing, certainly not a weapon. No blowgun."

Dana was totally confused. "I'm not sure where you're going with this, Sergeant. Are you trying to say that this blowgun, which you claim was found in my room, was the weapon that killed Louis?"

"I cannot positively say that. But here are the facts. A dart from a blowgun killed Monsieur Bertrand. Such a gun was found in your room. And you deny any knowledge of it."

"I certainly do!" Dana's confusion had turned to anger. "Your accusation is absurd. I hardly knew Louis Bertrand and had no reason to kill him, certainly not with a blowgun. I've never touched such a weapon, never even seen one. As far as I'm concerned, this interview is over."

She started to get to her feet, only to be stopped by a quick move from the aide, whom Kantana controlled with a nod of his head.

"This is...ludicrous," Dana insisted, even as she sat back down, adding defiantly, "you're accusing the wrong person, and you're going to be very sorry."

He raised skeptical eyebrows. "Oh, do you think so? I show you further evidence, mademoiselle." He placed a stack of notebooks and papers on the desk. "Detailed notes on the Pygmies. It would seem that you came very well prepared."

Dana's anger was replaced by a deep dread. "Those are my father's notes. He knew about the Pygmies, not I."

"But you brought them with you," Kantana said smoothly.

"That was my choice." She felt suddenly invaded, and she refused to put up with it.

"Not if murder was the result. Now tell me, why did you bring the notes with you?"

Dana chose her words carefully. "I am a language teacher, a professor specializing in rare and exotic tongues. For that reason, my father's work with the Mgembe interested me. When I had a chance to travel a route he'd taken years before, naturally, I jumped at the opportunity." She lifted her chin defiantly. "There's nothing illegal about that."

"Certainly not," Kantana agreed. "But it is interesting, to say the least, that both you and Monsieur Bertrand shared a fascination with the Mgembe, that you carried with you notebooks filled with information on the Pygmies, and that he was killed in a way that they are known to murder." He held up the weapon.

"I didn't have a blowgun—either that one or any other!" she cried adamantly. "We've just arrived here. Where would I have found one?" She knew the answer to that question even before it was out of her mouth.

"In the market. When you went shopping with Mademoiselle Kittredge. She tells me that you were not together throughout that trip."

"Well, no, we weren't. I was tired and—" Dana realized that the overly friendly Millicent had passed on information that could seem incriminating. "But I didn't buy a blowgun then or ever. Even if I had, how do you suggest I poisoned the tip?"

"The poison is also readily available, alas," he replied with apparent sadness.

"And of course, I know exactly how to administer it," she said sarcastically.

Kantana placed his hand on top of her father's notebooks. "It is all here, easy for a clever woman to understand. Indeed, you are a clever woman."

Dana didn't like the insinuation in his voice. "Someone planted that blowgun in my room."

Kantana shrugged, seemingly no longer interested in the topic. "I also have corroborating information that you and Monsieur Bertrand became very close friends during your voyage on the *Congo Queen*. Do you deny that you spent much time together?"

More incriminating information, this time from Betty's mouth, which didn't surprise Dana in the slightest. She *was* surprised about Millicent's betrayal, though. So much for the support of her fellow tourists.

"Louis and I spent time together," she answered finally, "but he was with Father Theroux much more often. Why don't you question him?"

"As I mentioned, I intend to," Kantana said coolly "But of course that is my business, the concern of the authorities. Now I ask again, could it be possible that there was a romance of some kind between you and Bertrand? Something that might have caused you to quarrel with him—"

"And to kill him? No, Sergeant. No! The idea is absurd. And you said yourself that you needed a motive—"

"Motive, means and opportunity," Kantana said, quoting his own earlier remarks. "The latter two, we have established, have we not?"

"No, I—"

"Of course, you had both the means," he said, touching the blowgun, "and the opportunity. You knew Louis was alone by the river, and you could have approached without alarming him. And of course, you were the last person to be seen with the victim." He heaved a satisfied sigh. "Further, I now realize that you are an expert on the Mgembe, who have made the blowgun into an art form."

He settled back comfortably, crossed his arms over his chest and waited for her to respond.

That's when Dana realized that she was caught up in a nightmare too horrible for her to contemplate. It couldn't be happening, but it was. "You believe I'm guilty," she blurted out.

He didn't respond. His face was expressionless.

She suddenly realized was was happening. Kantana was going to arrest her!

Dana struggled to keep her voice calm. "I demand to talk to a lawyer."

He almost chuckled. "There is no lawyer in Porte Ivoire, mademoiselle."

"Then I demand my phone call. Surely, even here, an accused person gets at least one call. I want to talk to the American Embassy in Brazzaville."

"This is not the United States, Mademoiselle. French law is somewhat different from yours. And as much as I would like to oblige you with a phone call, there are no phones in Porte Ivoire."

"Then use the shortwave radio on the boat," Dana demanded.

"I shall do this much for you," Kantana said in noxious tones. "After I interview Father Theroux, I shall send him to talk with you in jail—"

"Jail? No!" Dana was on her feet. "You can't do that. You can't put me in jail—not on circumstantial evidence. You're insane. You're—"

She saw his face then. Cold, hard, implacable.

"I'm not guilty of this horrible crime," she said. "I'm not guilty!"

He sat watching wordlessly.

"Why don't you look where the guilt really lies." She leaned forward, her hands on his desk, and spoke carefully with all the confidence she could muster. "It belongs on Alex Jourdan."

As soon as Dana made that statement, she realized her total belief in it. His obnoxious behavior last night had sent her rushing into Louis's arms—almost as if the whole meeting had been arranged—by Alex. And today, he'd been watchful, mysterious, not just dangerous, but possibly deadly. She'd been suspicious from the beginning. Now she knew why.

"Listen to me," she demanded. "Alex and Louis were on the outs. Something had gone wrong between them. Everyone knew that. And I overheard them just last night, arguing about a deal of some kind. I heard them!"

"And did anyone else hear this argument, mademoiselle?"

"I don't know. But everyone was aware of the bad blood between Alex and Louis. You can't deny that," she said firmly.

Kantana didn't flinch. "I, as everyone else, knew of the bad blood between the two men. As for the recent argument, which you say that you overheard, Alex told me that he had warned Bertrand to stay away from *you*, Mademoiselle. It is unfortunate, is it not, that Bertrand did not listen to the warning?"

The edges of the room grew fuzzy, and Kantana and his aide faded in and out of focus. She wasn't going to faint, but Dana thought she might be sick. She grasped the arms of the chair and sank into it, her head reeling.

"Things like this don't happen to people like me," she said slowly. "I'm a tourist, a college professor. I've never been arrested, never even gotten a traffic ticket." She looked at Kantana pleadingly. "People like me don't commit murder!"

Kantana shook his head sadly. "All kinds of people commit murder, mademoiselle."

Dana couldn't think of a response. She sat immobile before him as Kantana rose slowly and spoke to her in soft tones.

"And now, mademoiselle, I shall ask my aide to escort you to our local jail. There, we shall do all in our power to make you comfortable."

STRANGELY, no one was around when the American was taken away. But I was watching. I suspect that everyone was watching.

Dana's being with Louis that night had been a stroke of luck, and hiding the blowgun in her room had been an impulsive but brilliant decision. It put all the focus on her and away from the real reason behind his murder.

She'd been easy for me to set up. She knew no one; she had no connections. Justice moved slowly in the Congo, and someday she might be found innocent. But by then it wouldn't matter. My game would be over.

Chapter Three

Alex was settled comfortably in his favorite rattan chair on the veranda, drinking a beer, contemplating the river and wondering what the hell he was going to do about his life. He didn't look up when Maurice Longongo appeared; instead, he balanced the chair on its two back legs as was his habit and propped his foot against the porch rail.

"I hear they've made an arrest," Longongo said in his precise voice.

Alex didn't respond immediately, but that didn't seem to bother the government official, who persisted. "The American is in jail even as we speak."

"We're not speaking, Longongo. *You're* speaking," Alex clarified.

"In any case, the woman is in jail."

"Kantana thinks he has evidence," Alex said brusquely, trying to cut off further conversation.

Longongo wasn't discouraged. He perched on a chair beside Alex. "She hardly knew Bertrand."

Alex shrugged.

"I cannot fathom a motive," Longongo persisted.

"Who can figure women out? I sure as hell can't. If I were you, I'd leave it alone. Let the policeman do his work."

Longongo's eyes narrowed cunningly as he wet his lips with the tip of his tongue. "It seems a coincidence, doesn't it, that so many of us on the *Queen* were also at the Egyptian's party in Brazzaville?"

Alex took a final swig of his beer and tossed the bottle into a nearby trash can. "Were you?" he said, barely stifling a yawn.

"Yes. A most elegant party at a large estate outside the city. I was there as a government representative, of course. Poor Louis was there also, as a merchant. I believe he supplied the wine through one of his contacts. Miss Kittredge and Miss Weston and her companion were guests, as well. Then we all turned up as passengers on the *Queen*. And now here we all are in Porte Ivoire."

"Life is filled with strange coincidences, Longongo. Like the American woman's knowledge of the Mgembe." Alex got to his feet. "However, I'm tired of hearing about Louis and about the woman. What I need is another beer."

He stepped into the hotel bar, leaving Longongo sitting alone in the hot afternoon sun.

THERE WERE TWO cells in the Port Ivoire jail. Only one of them was occupied. Dana sat on the side of a rickety cot, still stunned, unbelieving, almost paralyzed with fury. How dare they! She stood up and paced the eight-by-eight-foot space. The jail, and her abysmal cell, could have been a symbol for all the deterioration of Porte Ivoire.

She knew something about the town from her reading, even more from her trip into the marketplace yesterday. And she'd seen the rest on her incredible journey today from the hotel to the jail under a police escort that consisted of one ridiculous aide to Kantana and the sergeant himself.

She sat back down. What a place to be incarcerated! Once the town had been a major trading post on the Congo, shipping out ivory for the craftsmen of the East and Europe, and animals for the zoos of the world. International laws and changing mores had put an end to that, and as an environmentalist, Dana was glad of it.

But the result was a town sliding into lassitude, a place on the verge of extinction. It lay somnambulant on the bank of the river, its buildings rotting, worn down by tropical heat and humidity, its population gradually drifting away to larger cities downriver, its market the last gasp of enterprise.

The jail to which she'd been so summarily whisked away was testament to the town's failure. A pitiful concrete block building, it stood on a dusty side street in the most neglected section of the town, Kantana's office in front, the two cells behind. In her cell were a cot, basin and chamber pot. There was one window, about four feet off the ground, its bars rusted but still strong enough to keep her inside. Through the window, vines and bushes pushed against the jail as if the jungle were hungry to reclaim what had once belonged to it.

Not surprisingly, there was no screen across the window, and insects buzzed freely in and out, making their homes in the crevices of the walls. Soon it would be dark, and the mosquitoes would begin their invasion. It seemed absurd that she was even worried about the mosquitoes, but she could be sure they would come. She could only speculate on what else to look forward to.

Her first hope had been centered on Father Theroux. She'd expected his visit from the moment she landed in the cell, and it had finally come after more than two hours. He brought food and prayers but little in the way of encouragement.

"You know I shall do whatever possible," he said, standing uneasily by the door.

"Then please intervene with Kantana for me. Your word will carry weight with him."

"Oh, I'm afraid that is not the case, my child." The priest fixed his gaze on the scene out the window as if he didn't want to meet her eyes. "I have known Jean Luc for many years, and he has always been a very decisive, even stubborn man. Not in the least likely to change his mind."

"That's ridiculous," Dana snapped. "Sorry." She didn't want to offend him so she chose her next words more carefully. "But as an officer of the law, he has to pay attention to evidence and testimony—"

"And I imagine he would profess to have done just that. The blowgun was in your room."

Dana's heart plummeted at the finality of Father Theroux's hard words spoken in such a gentle tone. "I'm innocent, Father!"

"Of course, you are, my dear. But Jean Luc can only act on the evidence at hand."

"Then he has to look again. And again!"

"Yes, of course." The priest hesitantly assured her, "I'll speak to him."

"Thank you, Father." She leaned against the cell wall. As if the priest's mild words would change the sergeant's mind or convince him to reopen the investigation.

"Jean Luc is an intelligent man," Theroux said, further discouraging her, "who usually knows what he's doing."

"Well, he doesn't know this time. Unless he's framing me on purpose," Dana shot back. She stood up straight and looked at the priest with narrowed eyes, a spark of hope flaming momentarily. "Maybe he's part of the setup. Maybe he's framing me to . . . to protect himself! He could have killed Louis as easily as anyone else!"

"Oh, no." The priest shook his head in distress. "Jean Luc is totally honorable. I can't imagine—"

"Well, I can," Dana interrupted. "The law isn't above corruption. When I get a lawyer, I'm going to have him investigate Kantana, who is just as likely to be guilty as I."

Father Theroux's smile was gentle. "We are all guilty of many things, in many ways," he said profoundly. "And now, before I leave, let us pray that the Lord will rid us of our unfounded guilt . . ."

"And punish those on whom the guilt is not unfounded," Dana added.

The priest opened one eye and looked at her forgivingly as Dana closed her eyes and prayed.

He left her with a crock of cooked chicken, a Bible and some information that stunned her. Louis was to be buried in Porte Ivoire—and Alex Jourdan was paying for the funeral!

DANA WASN'T HUNGRY but forced herself to eat the chicken and rice. It was all Father Theroux left; certainly no hope. So she ate the food. It was either that or fight the roaches and ants for it later in the evening. She had just finished when she heard a familiar voice echoing in the hall.

"This place is disgustingly dirty! Someone needs to get in here with a mop and scrub brush."

Dana caught a glimpse of Sergeant Kantana making a quick escape into his office and out of Millicent's way as she breezed by, her face red from the heat and her gray hair standing out in tufts around her face. To Dana she looked like an angel of mercy. A lot more decisive than the good Father.

"Oh, Millie, thank heavens you're here. Did you get through to the American Embassy in Brazzaville? I asked Father Theroux to remind you, but who knows where his head was when he left here. So what happened? Did you talk to them, did you—"

"Calm yourself, Dana. Take a deep breath and slow down. Getting overwrought won't help anything," Millicent ordered.

"Overwrought? You're damned right, I'm overwrought. Look around! I'm in jail, Millicent, in case you haven't noticed. Sergeant Kantana has taken all my money and my passport, and I'm being held for murder. Murder, Millicent! It's enough to make anyone overwrought. Besides which, Father Theroux offered me no encouragement whatsoever."

"He can be somewhat ineffectual," Millicent agreed.

"Ineffectual? He mouthed accusations that came straight from the sergeant."

"Like?"

"Like a blowgun was found in my room. I'm not a complete idiot, Millicent."

"No, indeed, you're not."

"And only a fool would kill someone and then keep the murder weapon in her room. I would have thrown it in the river, for God's sake."

"Of course," Millicent agreed. "And as for your supposed love affair with Louis on board the *Queen*—"

"There was nothing between me and Louis. I was probably less friendly to him than anyone—except Alex." Dana leaned her forehead against the bars of her cell. "To make things more confusing, Father Theroux tells me Alex has offered to pay the funeral expenses."

"Well, obviously, in this heat, the body can't be returned to Brazzaville."

"That's not the point, Millicent. The point is, he's paying—Alex, who was supposedly Louis's enemy." Dana covered her face with her hands. "This is so awful. I can't even believe the man is dead, much less that I'm accused of killing him! It's like a terrible nightmare."

Millicent patted Dana's hand that grasped the cell bar. "I'm sure things will work out once I get through to the American Embassy," she said soothingly.

"You haven't reached them yet?" Dana was dismayed.

"The radio is down on the *Congo Queen*. Just temporary, I'm sure."

Dana beat her fists ineffectually against the bars. "What kind of a place is this? No phones, no lawyers, no working radios..."

"It's the Congo, dear. That's just the way things are. And you must accept it—at least for a while."

Dana gave her a hard look. "Not on your life. I'm going to fight like crazy, Millie, and I need your help."

"You'll have it, I guarantee. After all, I'm the leader of this tour, and I feel responsible. For everyone," she added quickly. "Are they treating you well?"

Dana gave a bitter laugh. "Look around. I'm sharing a cell with half the insect life of Central Africa. I'm locked in a space eight feet square with no running water. I've only been here a couple of hours, but I can assure you that I'm not being treated well."

Millicent pushed a bundle through the bars. "I brought you some fresh clothes."

"Thanks," Dana said, taking the clothes and tossing them on the cot. She suddenly lost her spunk and felt the tears building. Slowly, they trickled down her cheeks.

"We'll think of something," Millicent assured her. "I'll talk to Kantana."

"Please," Dana begged. "Ask him to let me out. Father Theroux says I can come to the mission until the investigation is over. I won't try to escape," she said a little pitifully.

"I'm sure you won't."

"And when you get through to the embassy, have someone call my brothers in Colorado. Kurt and Andy will fly right over. Do you have something to write on? I'll give you their numbers."

Millicent produced a pencil and notebook, and Dana wrote down the information. She had no doubt they'd drop everything and come to Africa as soon as they heard about her plight. Dana and her brothers had become even closer after the death of their parents. Nothing would keep them from helping her.

"Now, what else?" Millicent asked sympathetically. "Father Theroux brought you dinner..."

"Yes, and promises my next meal. Well, I don't intend to be in here that long."

"And I'm sure you won't, my dear." Millicent offered another pat.

"Meanwhile, Betty has a real hook for her story—'Murder in the Congo, America teacher arrested.' I can just see it—"

"That slut," Millicent said emphatically.

Dana did a double take, not believing her ears. Admittedly, Millicent was an outspoken woman, but Dana never had heard such a remark from the Englishwoman's lips.

"That's just what she is," Millicent reinforced.

"I thought you liked her. You invited her on the cruise—"

Millicent waved a dismissive hand. "I ran into her at a party and felt a momentary empathy because she was out of work."

"Well, she's working now," Dana said sarcastically. "Just keep her away from me. I can't be responsible for what I might do."

"Admittedly, I made a mistake bringing her on the tour. Her behavior with Yassif has been disgusting."

Again, Dana was surprised at the emotion in Millicent's voice. "Hardly to be compared with murder," she snapped.

Millicent's eyes brightened behind her thick glasses. "Do you think Betty—"

"No," Dana said firmly. "There's only one viable suspect, and that's Alex."

Millicent was thoughtful. "I've known Alex for a long time, and I understand what he's capable of. A little larceny here and there, lying when it suits him, womanizing, it goes without saying. But murder—"

Dana felt a burst of anger. "I don't believe this! No one wants to admit that Alex could be guilty—not you, not Father Theroux, certainly not Kantana. In spite of the fact that the man's practically a criminal. Whereas everyone immediately assumes I'm guilty when I'm the least likely person in the world to commit murder."

"But you, my dear girl, are a stranger here." Millicent's response, meant to be kind, sent cold chills down Dana's spine. "The rest of us know one another, our capabilities as well as our frailties, while you are an unknown element. Of course, you'd be an obvious suspect."

Dana felt sick. She was a stranger in a far-off land—with no one to stand up for her, no one to take her side. "You will help me, won't you?" she asked in a shaky voice.

Millicent's voice was strong and reassuring. "Of course. I'll get on it right now. I'll keep after that captain until he gets the radio working."

"Thank you." Dana couldn't keep the tremble out of her voice.

NIGHT FELL over Porte Ivoire like a thick, heavy cloak. Strangely, as I'd noticed often, the darkness didn't muffle sound; noises seemed to intensify. The beating wings of a raptor swooping down on its prey; the rustle of a night animal in dry grass; the rumble of laughter from the waterfront. It had been that way the night Louis died. All the sounds magnified. I remember distinctly the whisper of the dart. The sharp intake of Louis's breath. The sound of his body falling across the path.

Too bad he had to die. He had such a love for life, for fine wine and good food. And women. Most of them

*fell for his world-weary, French dilettante line. Few
women knew what Louis was really like or what he was
up to.*

DANA PUT ON the clean slacks and shirt Millicent
brought and tried not to be intimidated by the darkness that was creeping into her cell. It was hard to ignore when the animals outside increased their frantic
calling. And the shadows lengthened . . . her heartbeat
accelerated.

It was the rapid beating of her heart that told Dana
she was in trouble; getting through the night was going
to be hell, and she wasn't sure she was prepared for it.

Kantana made a last visit before leaving for home and
dinner. Victor, his aide, was left in charge. And that was
not comforting, particularly when he came to the office door every few minutes and looked down the hall
at her. After the third time, she crawled onto her bed in
the corner of the cell, out of his view.

The black night was illuminated by a single bulb
swaying in the hall, casting its crazy shadows on Dana.

I could die here, she thought.

And the only thing that could prevent her death
would be action on Dana's part. She needed a plan of
some kind. But what? She had no money, no passport.
She couldn't even bribe her jailer!

Dana drew her legs to her chest and tried to make
herself into a little ball. Tried to disappear. She was too
tired to think and too scared to sleep. Tears began to
trickle down her cheeks. She felt alone and very sorry
for herself.

Against her will, she dozed off. Voices awoke her, two
men speaking French in whispers. She couldn't make
out what they were saying. It seemed like déjà vu, that

conversation, so similar to what she heard—or thought she heard—between Alex and Louis that fateful night.

Then it was quiet, and she heard only the noises of the night, those terrifying sounds that kept her on edge, huddled on the bed, ready for anything.

"I wonder how many stars Louis would have given this place?"

The voice came from the window, and at the sound of it, Dana bolted to her feet. "Who is it?" she cried. Then she saw his face, briefly, as the bulb cast a quick illumination on the cell window.

"Alex Jourdan! What the hell are you doing here?"

"Keep your voice down," he ordered, "so Victor doesn't hear you. Wait until he turns the tape recorder on. There . . ." he said as the music wafted from the jail office.

Dana listened for a moment to the sound of jazz. "You brought him a tape recorder?"

"Sure. He loves jazz. I brought him some beer, too. that'll help him pass the hours while he guards his dangerous prisoner."

Dana shot him a long, hate-filled look. "Are you crazy?"

"I needed to talk with you. The jazz and the beer will give me that chance, keep him occupied while you and I make a deal."

"A deal? You *are* insane! There's no way I'm dealing with Louis's murderer. Now get away from the window or I'll scream for Victor."

"No, you won't," Alex said calmly. "You'll listen to what I have to say because, lady, I'm your only hope."

"Then God pity me," Dana said flatly, "if I have to depend on the likes of you." She moved into the corner and climbed onto her bed, as far away from him as she could get. Even though he was on the other side of the bars, she felt safer away from the window.

"You don't have to depend on me," he said, "but I think you'll want to when you hear what I can do."

"And just what is that?" Dana asked.

"I can break you out of this place," he answered in a hoarse whisper.

"Don't be ridiculous," she replied loudly.

"Be quiet or I'll never get a chance to show you. I can get you out of here now. Tonight. We can cross the border into Zaire and then fly to Kenya. You can go to the American Embassy, get a new passport and be out of this part of the world before Jean Luc gets organized enough to put together a chase. You can be free, Dana."

Free. The word sounded wonderful, but there was no way freedom would come from Alex Jourdan. There was no way she could trust him.

"Come here, Dana. I don't want to shout. Come here so I can tell you what I have in mind."

Curiosity got the best of her. Whatever he had to say, listening to him would be preferable to cowering uselessly. She went to the window. When she was within two feet of him, she stopped.

"Come closer," he urged.

"No, this is good enough."

"What I have to say is for no ears but yours. If you don't come close, I can't speak."

Warily, she approached. She was obviously the crazy one for even talking to him. Their encounter in the garden the night before, the perplexing mixture of emotions it aroused in her, was all too immediate. She didn't just remember those feelings; she felt them. Attraction. Excitement. Anger. And danger; it had been there in the garden, and it was here in the jail.

But she'd already taken the first step toward him. She took another. His face was in shadow, but she could make out his features in the dim light. The look in his eyes was dark and intense, and the seductive whisper of his voice drew her on.

"I can help you, Dana."

She kept her voice low. "You don't strike me as the altruistic type. There must be something in this for you."

He flashed a smile, and she caught a glimpse of his even, white teeth. "No, I'm not altruistic. Let's put it this way. I'm meeting a mutual need. But I can't explain unless I can see you. Step a little closer, into the moonlight."

Dana hesitated. She knew Alex was a charlatan and a rogue with the ability to draw people into his orbit, use and discard them. But in spite of the peril surrounding him, Alex had her attention. She felt a connection with him, something intangible but powerful, that kept her senses whirling. He was manipulating her. She knew that, but she didn't know why.

"Just one more step," he urged.

Common sense warned her to keep her distance, but hope tugged fiercely. Should she risk listening to him? Yes! a voice inside told her. Maybe he really could help her. And dammit, she was intrigued. She stepped to the window.

"Good," he said. "Now I can see you clearly." His eyes softened. "This experience has taken its toll. You look worn-out, Dana."

"Don't bother with the sympathy, Alex," she snapped. "Just tell me why you're here." She wasn't going to get emotionally entangled with him. That could be as deadly as being locked in the Porte Ivoire jail.

He grinned sardonically at her brusqueness. "Okay, here's the bargain. I need to get out of the country; so do you. I know how to stay alive in the bush, and you know how to deal with the Pygmies. We can get out together."

"Oh, no," she said. "I'm not going anywhere with you, Alex Jourdan."

"Just hear me out. Zaire is the logical destination, and to get there, it's necessary to cross the Mgembe territory. You and Louis were among the few people who had knowledge of the Mgembe. Now he's gone. I need you to help me communicate with them."

"Communicate? I can't speak the language," she said flatly. "So if that's all there is to your bargain, then good night."

"Wait," he said. "Maybe you can't speak to them, but you can learn. You have tapes, notebooks. You know as much as Louis and a hell of a lot more than I do. You can do it."

"No," Dana repeated adamantly. As the sound of melodious American jazz drifted toward them on the hot humid night air, she began to put two and two together.

"You can talk to them, get them to take us to the border," Alex persisted.

She listened to the song, a familiar New Orleans jazz melody that she'd heard often years ago. It only added to the unreality of her situation. Arrested for murder. Held in a squalid jail, listening to a proposition from a man who was probably the real murderer while in the background a haunting piece of American music played. It took her another moment to review his proposal before the answer came to her.

"You and Louis were only pretending to be angry with each other!"

His silence confirmed her remark.

"You two had some kind of deal going—illegal, I imagine—and you needed to flee the country together. He was your contact with the Pygmies."

"Yes, in fact—"

"But then you argued—for real," Dana said suddenly. She felt as if a cold finger had touched the back of her neck. "You killed him," she whispered. "I'm sure of it now. You murdered him over the deal, and now more than ever you need to get out of the Congo."

"You're partly right. I do need to get out of here, but I didn't kill Louis. He was one of the best friends I ever had."

His voice had the ring of honesty, but she didn't believe him. A man like Alex Jourdan was obviously an accomplished liar.

Alex saw the look of disbelief flicker across her face. She was bright, there was no denying that. She'd caught on quickly to his deal with Louis. How long would it take her to catch on to the rest? He decided to change his approach, to let her believe she was in on the scheme. "I'm going to trust you, Dana, because I have to." He paused dramatically.

She said nothing.

"Louis and I did have a deal going, but not the kind you think. He was an agent of the French government, and certain documents had come into his hands—"

"Louis? An agent?"

"Think about it. He had the perfect cover. A dilettante with his finger in many pies, a man who knew everyone."

Standing there in the tiny cell listening to what seemed like an absurd tall tale from a possible killer on the other side of the barred window, Dana couldn't believe any of this was happening. But it was. And she'd better pay attention. What Alex said about Louis could be true. He'd been an extremely sophisticated man, with contacts at all levels of society. Maybe, just maybe...

"But why would he be hanging out with a lowlife like you?"

Alex laughed softly. "Unlike some people, whose view of me seems pretty tainted, Louis knew he could trust me. My job was to organize our trip out of the Congo. We were a good team."

She looked at him. Even in the dim light, she could see an expression on his face that seemed thoughtful, even sad. But he was an actor—and a scoundrel. "What kind of documents?" she asked skeptically.

"That's highly classified," Alex answered.

"What a surprise," she said sarcastically.

"I can tell you a part of it, and you can believe me or not." His voice was even lower, and she had to strain just to hear him.

"Louis learned that insurgents within the Congo are plotting to destabilize French oil interests in the country. Terrorist attacks, that kind of thing. It could bring economic and social chaos. The documents tell the whole story, and with Louis dead, I need to get them out of the country and into the right hands. Fast."

She was watching him intently, not so cynical now. He was close, Alex thought. He almost had her.

"So why didn't he just fly from Brazzaville to Paris? Surely that would have been easier than trekking through the jungle depending on Pygmies—"

"Not so loud," he warned her, buying a little time to frame an answer.

She looked toward the office where the music continued. "No one can hear us over the music, and the man doesn't understand English."

"That's where you're wrong. His English is excellent."

"All right," she said softly. "What about the airport as a way out?"

"It was being watched by the other side, Dana. Louis had powerful enemies. We'd hoped this river cruise would be the perfect cover. He'd stay at the hotel a few days, like a ordinary tourist. Then one night, we'd just take off. Obviously someone knew he had the documents and followed him."

"You mean someone on the boat—at the hotel—could be in the pay of the insurgents?"

"Any one of them," Alex answered. "They were all in Brazzaville with Louis. One of them could have caught on to what he was doing—"

"Or maybe," Dana interrupted with another thought, "whoever killed Louis wanted the papers for himself. Are they worth money?"

Alex nodded. "To the French government as well as to the insurgents."

"Where are the documents now?"

"Louis hid them in Father Theroux's luggage on the trip and then passed them to me. I have them."

Suddenly, Louis's behavior on the *Queen* made sense. He'd been protecting the documents. She looked sharply at Alex. "Maybe once you had the papers in your hands, you killed him."

"And left myself without a guide to get me the hell out of this place? No, I'm not that stupid, Dana. I needed Louis, and I never wanted him dead. He was my friend," Alex added.

"But someone on that boat murdered him. I gather you don't think it was me?"

Alex shrugged.

"Then who? Betty, Yassif, Millie, Father Theroux." She ran through the names quickly. "Longongo! He works for the government; he'd have inside information."

She was wavering now, wanting to believe. He applied more pressure. "Unlike you, I don't have time to play detective. I'm leaving tonight. With the documents. If you come with me, the trip will be easier and faster." He leaned closer, his voice a seductive whisper. "In a week, we could be in Nairobi."

It sounded insane to her, taking off through the jungle with a man who was untrustworthy at best and a killer at worst. A dark thought played in her mind. Maybe he wanted her dead! Maybe he'd break her out of jail just to kill her. "I don't know—"

"If you stay here, the situation is hopeless," Alex said flatly. "For one thing, Louis's killer might come after you. Have you thought of that?"

Dana shrank back against the wall of her damp, dank cell. She hadn't thought of it, and the possibility was frightening.

"If not the killer, one of the guards. Victor is the best of the bunch, but a couple of the others are nothing but thugs."

She *had* thought about that; it was just about all she'd thought about since Kantana put her in the cell. Victor was bad enough. Now she learned there were others even worse. She tried to grasp a semblance of hope. "Millie is going to get in touch with the American Embassy in Brazzaville, and someone there will call my brothers—" She struggled to keep her voice calm.

"Has Millie put in the call yet?"

"Well, no. The radio on the boat is down. Or something. She's trying. I think." Dana's words proved her despair.

"Don't hold your breath," Alex said. "Who knows when the radio will be repaired? They're still waiting for engine parts. So the radio is low priority. Once she does reach the embassy, if that ever happens, it'll take days for your brothers to get here. As you know, it's a hell of a long trip up the Congo to Porte Ivoire. A lot can happen in that time, Dana. You can rot here in jail, alone. I expect you've heard about tourists jailed in foreign countries. Some of them stay locked up for years."

"But this is different. I'm innocent!"

"Maybe."

"Alex, you said yourself—"

"Did I? I don't remember committing to your innocence."

He was right. When she'd declared her innocence, he'd just shrugged. But Dana had been so intent upon naming the real killer that she'd forged ahead, not noticing.

"Kantana is sure you're guilty. And if you are, I'm taking a hell of a chance making this offer."

"I'm not guilty, and I don't understand why no one believes me."

"Why should they? They don't know a damned thing about you except you seem to have an inordinate interest in Pygmies—and their methods of killing."

"You bastard," she said through clenched teeth. "You know damned well that I didn't kill Louis."

"Maybe you're innocent, and maybe you're not. But I'm the bastard who can get you out of here. Just think, Dana. Within a week you and I could be in Nairobi where there're great hotels. With hot water. Bathtubs. Thick, thick towels. Room service."

Dana's head pounded, and she rubbed her temples with the tips of her fingers. A week. Only a week, and she could be free of this nightmare. It could take that long before Millie even got through to the embassy. More delay before Dana's brothers arrived. Anything could happen to her during a week's time. She was vulnerable. Alone.

Yet she was afraid of Alex, too. His story was too glib and well thought out. She could imagine Louis being an agent, but Alex . . .

"Why do you give a damn about the documents?" she asked. "You don't seem any more patriotic than you are altruistic."

"I'll be well paid for my troubles. Money is a powerful motivator."

That made sense to Dana; that sounded like Alex.

"But I need you. I need your help with those damned Pygmies." His voice was low, pleading. "Please, Dana. For both of us. I swear I'll take care of you. I won't hurt you."

"The sergeant took all my notes." She could feel herself weakening.

"I'll get them," he said. "It'll only take a minute for me to handle Victor."

She panicked. "Stop. I didn't say for sure—"

"There's really no choice, Dana. You know it. I know it." He gave her a long, meaningful look. "Remember, I told you in the garden that I was waiting for you."

Dana felt the hairs along her neck prickle. He was waiting for her. Just as, in some unexplainable way, she'd been waiting for him. No, she told herself. She wouldn't accept that this was preordained. It was a nightmare, not a fantasy come to life. "Wait. I'm not sure, I—"

He was gone.

Dana rushed to the door of her cell. She heard the music. Nothing else. Then, suddenly, there were voices, the sound of a scuffle. What if Victor overpowered Alex—and then took his anger out on her? What had she gotten herself into? She clutched the bars of her cell so tightly that her nails dug into her palms.

There was a loud crash. Then the music stopped. Everything was quiet. She hung on to the bars and waited. Footsteps headed toward her down the hall. She squinted into the darkness but could see nothing. Perspiration dripped down her forehead. She clung to the bars, paralyzed.

Then Alex appeared. He was carrying a canvas satchel. He dropped it on the floor. "Your Pygmy notes, safe and sound." He unlocked the cell and pushed open the door.

Dana hesitated.

Alex reached through the door and grasped her arm. "Come on. We need to be on our way before sunrise."

She took a step forward and then stopped.

"Dana. Think about the alternative."

She'd already thought about it, and there was no choice. He was right. She stepped through the open cell door and followed him down the hall. They passed Victor, who lay on the floor, eyes closed, wrists handcuffed behind him. She stopped, looking down. But Alex pulled her along with him. "He won't be out long. I didn't hurt him."

They pushed through the sagging screen door and onto the street. Dana had time for one long breath of fresh air before Alex hustled her into a Jeep. "We make a quick trip to the hotel for your gear. Then we're on our way."

She sat beside him in the Jeep, not really believing what had happened. But it was too late to change her mind. For good or ill, she and Alex Jourdan were in this together.

Chapter Four

Alex stopped the Jeep in the shadows of a giant gum tree. The hotel and all its inhabitants appeared to be locked in a deep slumber. Only one faint light gleamed from an upstairs window.

"Do you suppose Sergeant Kantana left a guard?" Dana whispered.

Alex's lips twisted in a grin. "I suppose not."

"What gives you that—"

"Dana, trust me. There're no police on duty here. They're occupied elsewhere tonight. Kantana is at home with his family, our friend Victor is—well, you know where he is. The other two are out with their girlfriends. No one is guarding the hotel. Why should they? The prime suspect is supposedly behind bars."

"Then let's go inside," Dana said with what she hoped was enthusiasm.

"We'll have to make it fast," Alex warned. "Grab what you need—a change of clothes and antimalaria pills, antibiotics, painkillers—"

"You make this trip sound delightful."

"It's good sense to be prepared."

Dana shot him an amused look. While Alex Jourdan might be prepared, he was far from being a Boy Scout!

As Dana reached for the door handle, Alex put a restraining hand on her arm. "We still need to be careful. Anyone could see you and turn you back in to Kantana."

"Don't worry. I'll sneak quietly up to my room, fill my backpack and return here before you've finished getting your stuff."

"I've already finished," he told her. "The tents, supplies, food are in the back of the Jeep. So I'll keep you company."

She climbed out of the Jeep. "That's not necessary."

"Oh, yes, it is," he replied. "I'm not letting you out of my sight." He leaned close and whispered in her ear, "For instance, you might decide to make a run for the mission."

"No, I—" she began.

"And if you did, Father Theroux would probably give you sanctuary. Nope, we're sticking close to each other from now on." As he spoke the words, he leaned close for emphasis.

With a sigh, Dana followed him. Her mind was hard at work as they furtively crossed the garden, and when they reached the stairs that led to the second-floor balcony, she knew her plans were shot down. Of course, he'd been right. It had certainly crossed her mind to try to escape and run to Father Theroux. Whether or not she would have put the thought to action, Dana didn't know. Now she'd never find out. Alex's grip on her arm was firm. There was no breaking away.

She could call out and awaken someone. But if that person turned out to be Betty or Yassif or Longongo she'd be back at square one. Except this time Kantana would have no doubt of her guilt.

So unless something unforeseen happened, she and Alex were going to be a couple, no matter how ill-matched.

"HURRY UP," Alex ordered. "You're taking too long."

"What do you expect?" she retorted in a whisper. "I'm trying to pack in the dark." She crouched in front of her suitcase, transferring belongings into a back-pack, while he waited impatiently at the door to her hotel room.

She clumsily stuffed the last few items in the pack just as Alex decided he'd waited long enough.

"We're leaving now," he said. "Grab everything, and let's go."

Dana did as he ordered, stood up quickly, headed to the door—and bumped into a table. She reached out to steady it, but too late. The carved leopard she'd bought in the market slid off the table to the floor. To Dana the sound was deafening.

"Dammit," Alex cursed under his breath. "What're you doing?"

"It was an accident," she shot back as she replaced the leopard. "I'm ready now."

"Too late," Alex muttered as he reached out and grabbed her. "I hear Betty." He pulled her into the closet.

Dana started to object before she realized he was right. Betty was on the balcony, talking to her boy-friend. "Did you hear that, Yassif—a noise in Dana's room!"

Dana felt her heart pounding rapidly, like a frightened deer. Betty and Yassif—the two people she wanted most to avoid.

Alex's arm tightened around her waist as he held her close, grasping her so tightly that she couldn't move. Suddenly her fear was superceded by something else—the physical aspect of her situation. Their bodies were thrust close together, her face against his shoulder, her breasts pushed into his chest, her hips angled into his. She was vividly aware of his lean strength, the power of his arms, the way he held her, making her feel slight and small. And powerless.

The darkness of the closet was thick, impenetrable, intensifying every movement, every sensation. Alex's breathing, quick and hard, melded with her own. She was enveloped by the warmth of his body; it merged with hers. In the darkness, she couldn't be sure where he ended and she began. Overpowering fear merged with incredible desire, and both raced in her blood.

Alex could feel Dana's heart, thudding wildly against his chest, racing a mile a minute. She was scared as hell—and she should be. He wasn't thrilled over the situation himself, trapped in the closet with only one way out. But if he had to take on Yassif, he would.

That wasn't the entire problem, Alex realized as he forced himself to take slow, long breaths and concentrate on what was happening between Betty and her lover—not what was happening to his body, glued against Dana's.

It was a losing battle.

His shirt was unbuttoned halfway down his chest, and her breasts were soft and firm pressed against him. The agonizing touch of her nipples, taut against his bare skin, was more than he bargained for. But that couldn't compare with what was happening lower down where one of her legs was wedged against his thigh. He tried to ignore his body's reaction. But he couldn't ignore

Dana, her accelerated breathing, her hair tickling his chin, and most of all the lush fullness of her body in his arms.

Betty's voice reached them through the crack in the balcony door. Alex tensed and gave her his full attention. She was very close, just outside, and her words were clear and precise as she called out to Yassif.

"Maybe the noise wasn't from this room, but I still think we ought to check."

Yassif responded, sleepy and uninterested. And barely understandable. His first words were a jumble of languages. Then he yelled in English, "What? What?"

"I thought I heard something, darling."

"Is nothing," he answered. "Come back to bed."

"Maybe—" she began.

Alex held his breath. Damn the woman. He'd never known her to refuse an invitation to bed. He tightened his grip and prayed Dana wouldn't break yet. One sound could alert Betty. Seconds seemed like hours.

"Maybe you're right," Betty said finally to Yassif. "It could be a rat setting off a trap. This place is crawling with rodents."

Alex felt Dana relax against him, but he held her fast. They were far from safe.

Then Betty laughed, low and seductive. "There're better ways to spend the night than snooping about, my love."

Yassif's low grunt was followed by the sound of the balcony door closing. Alex didn't move. Dana tried to pull away from him, but he held tightly onto her. They would move when he was ready.

Then he *was* ready. And he didn't want to let her go. He wondered if the darkness and danger had affected her as it had him. He felt energized, alive, as if he'd run a race—and won. They'd been close to the edge, close to getting caught, but they'd made it together.

Dana's lips were only inches away in the darkness. He thought of kissing her, a long, hard kiss of victory, before they set out into the unknown. What would her lips taste like? He could find out very easily by bending down, taking her face in his hands, pressing his mouth to hers . . .

Dana couldn't understand why Alex wouldn't let her go. Betty and Yassif had returned to their room. It seemed safe, but he still held on to her, and his arms felt less like those of a captor than a lover.

She responded to the feeling as awareness flooded through her, wild and hot. His lean body insinuated itself even closer. Her skin against his felt flushed and hot. She drew a long shaky breath. This wasn't supposed to happen, she thought frantically, not feelings like this. Not with Alex Jourdan. She needed distance. And time. She needed light and air.

"You can let me go now," she whispered

Instead he willfully held her, even strengthened his grasp.

His stubbornness gave Dana the strength she needed, and her anger surfaced. He obviously wanted to show her that he was in control, that he could handle her, overpower her. But she wouldn't let him. Acting instinctively, Dana kicked out sideways and connected with his ankle.

He gave a gasp but held on. "I'll let you go when I think it's safe." His mouth was still close to hers; he hadn't given up his intent to kiss her, only postponed it.

Dana tried to twist her head away from him, but Alex held fast. "I can tell when it's safe as well as you."

"Maybe so, but you're the one who telegraphed our presence in the first place by knocking into the table."

Her lips tightened. "Why is everything with you a battle?"

"Because you make everything so damned difficult."

She bit back an angry retort. "Can we just get out of here?" Dana gritted her teeth when his answer didn't come immediately. Why did he insist on that take-charge attitude?

Finally, he dropped his arms. "Let's go."

She stepped out of the closet, but he held her back.

"I'll lead the way. After all, this is my hotel, and I know it best."

Instead of calling him the name he justly deserved and telling him what she thought about his arrogance, which was out of place in this situation, she censored her words and answered sweetly, if sarcastically. "Of course, Alex. I'm sure you always know best."

Inside she continued to seethe, not only at his high-handed behavior but at her inability to control her feelings about him. How much simpler it would be if she could only keep thinking of him as a liar, even a murderer, and hate him. But even though her feelings included distrust and fear, they also included emotions that had almost gotten out of control. It wouldn't happen again, she swore.

BY THE TIME they reached the Stanley Hotel's main staircase and began to creep silently down the steps, Dana was glad that Alex led the way, carrying her backpack. She followed, her hand on his shoulder, and prayed she wouldn't take a misstep in the dark. Anger at him aside, she realized they'd been within a hairbreadth of discovery by Betty and Yassif, and if that had happened . . .

She shuddered to think of herself back in that tiny, filthy cell. She would do anything to keep that from happening. She'd even follow Alex into the jungle.

Her foot came to rest on the last step, but before she could breath a sigh of relief, it creaked loudly. She froze and heard Alex mutter a curse. As if his hotel's squeaking stair was her fault!

After an interminable wait, he seemed to decide they were safe and moved toward the back of the hotel, across the kitchen and out into the night air, which was cool on their faces. Night birds called out from the trees, the sound of a million insects vibrated on the breeze, and Dana relaxed as they made their way toward the Jeep, hidden in the shadows.

Then Alex stopped short. *"Merde,"* he muttered. "That damned Longongo is out for a midnight walk."

He pulled her behind a palm tree, and from there they watched in frustration as Longongo strolled back and forth, almost aimlessly, his face turned upward, seemingly surveying the heavens, its stars large and improbably close.

Alex cursed again. "A damned stargazer," he whispered.

"Maybe he'll go back in soon," she offered.

"Soon? We have to get out of here now," he said in an angry whisper. "We can't wait. He has to be taken care of. When I get out of sight, make some noise, not too loud. And don't let him see you."

With that curt command, Alex merged into the shadows. Dana took a deep breath. He was an expert at giving orders, but when it came to adding details, he obviously lost interest. So there she was, alone in the Congo night, with orders to make noise.

She looked around and then picked up the backpack that he'd dropped silently at her feet. She closed her eyes, counted to three, threw it into the night and ducked back behind the tree.

Longongo stopped his stargazing and turned toward the sound while Dana froze behind the tree.

"*Qu'est-ce que c'est?* Who is there?"

Longongo moved toward the spot where the backpack had landed just as Alex emerged from the shadows behind him.

Dana heard a soft noise, a kind of sickening clunk. The little man slid soundlessly to the ground with Alex standing over him. He gestured to Dana, and she rushed out of hiding, stopping to pick up the pack.

"Is he—did you kill him?" she sputtered.

"I should have, but I didn't. Just a karate chop to the right spot. He's not seriously hurt, but he'll be out for a long time. Let's get moving."

They climbed into the Jeep, and Alex drove swiftly, without lights, depending on the light of the moon.

They reached the outskirts of Porte Ivoire, took a side road and picked up speed, skittering along, bumping over ruts, taking turns wildly as Dana held on for dear life.

"We're going away from the river," she called out finally as they careened along.

Alex didn't slow down as he explained. "The Congo makes a big loop here. We're heading for one of its tributaries, the Lomami."

"Is the Jeep amphibious?"

Alex glanced at her, registering surprise at her joke, just as they hit a bump.

She held on tight and added, "Or maybe you have a boat in your backpack?"

Alex laughed aloud. "You've got a sense of humor, but not a lot of respect, Dana. You should know that I have a plan. We're picking up a canoe at the next village."

"Then I'll just sit back and enjoy the ride," she said as they hit another pothole—whether accidentally or on purpose Dana couldn't be sure. His arrogance knew no bounds, but there was nothing she could do about it except hang on for the ride. She had to trust Alex. With her life in his hands, she had to depend on him. But how could she possibly depend on a man whom all of her instincts warned her not to trust?

As they bounced along, Dana thought about the warnings she'd gotten from Millicent and the others on the *Queen*. They'd told her that Alex was a ne'er-do-well living on the edge of the law. But according to the story he told her, he was the antithesis of those accusations—an upright man on a government mission of some kind, maybe even a professional agent. And the way he'd handled her jailbreak, taken care of the guard and Longongo with such dispatch, did have a professionalism about it.

But Dana had a much easier time thinking of him as a criminal. There was still the haunting memory of Louis's murder. Alex swore he was innocent, but what else could he say?

The Jeep hit another bump, and Dana grimaced at the jolt that shook her but said nothing. She'd wanted adventure when she came to the Congo. Now she was getting it —big time.

THEY DROVE into the village just ahead of the dawn. From the distance, Dana had a quick impression of sunbaked mud houses with thatched roofs, women in bright dresses bent over cooking pots and men carrying their fishing nets to the river. A sleepy village waking with the morning sun. Under different circumstances, she would have been thrilled to be here—an American tourist getting an inside look at an authentic African village.

Alex pulled the Jeep into a thatched palm shed behind an abandoned hut. "Stay here," he ordered. "Out of the way and quiet. I'm going to find my friend Gabriel. He has a boat ready for me."

"Why can't I get out?" she questioned. "I need to stretch my legs."

"The wrong person might see you," he commented flatly.

"Who? I don't know anyone here."

"Let's keep it that way." He looked at her critically in the faint light of the approaching dawn. Her hair hung limply around her face; her eyes were glazed from lack of sleep; her clothes were wrinkled. Disheveled and obviously exhausted, she was far different from the cool, elegant blonde who'd stepped off the *Congo Queen* just the day before.

"Okay," he agreed.

She started to step out of the Jeep.

"But wait. Do you have a kerchief—a scarf?"

"No. I have a hat—one of those crumpled khaki things."

"Does it cover your hair?"

"Well, yeah," she said, adding, "just about."

"Put it on and you can get out and walk around, but on the other side of the Jeep. And don't call attention to yourself. American blondes aren't an everyday occurrence around here, and the less of a trail we leave the better. I'll be back."

With that he strode off, making his way quickly down the hard-packed dirt road toward the village where Gabriel Butumo lived with his wife in one of the larger village huts. As Alex walked along, an occasional villager called out, and he waved a casual greeting. His presence here wasn't that unusual. Everyone knew that he and Gabriel were old friends. Alone, without Dana, he wasn't an oddity.

But she *was* here. And he wasn't sure whether that was a stroke of brilliance—or the worst move he'd ever made. He had no idea how much she really knew about the Mgembe. She might not even be able to make herself understood to them. Then what?

He shook away that thought. She knew enough, surely, to get them safely through Pygmy territory. He could do the rest; he could get them across the border. But to be certain, he needed something else. He needed Lady Luck firmly on his side.

That Lady had been playing tag with him from the beginning of this little episode, when Dana stepped off the boat with her precious notes on the Pygmies, which finally ended up in his hands. Now all he needed was for the Lady to stay by him, for his luck to hold out just a little while longer....

"Hey, Jourdan. What the hell are you doing out here so damned early?"

Alex grimaced at the sound of the Irish accent, not at all lilting in the early morning air. The voice belonged to Mac McQuire, and the sound of it could very well mean that his luck was running out.

"You're up early yourself, Mac," Alex replied without answering the question.

"Too damned hot to sleep." The Irishman left the shade of the porch where he'd been drinking his first whiskey of the morning and joined Alex. The guide's graying blond hair was pulled back in an untidy ponytail. His face was red from the sun, and his arms and hands were covered with freckles. He was stocky and well built, a real bull of a man. Alex knew from personal experience that Mac was tough as nails—and nobody's fool. That was necessary for a man if he was going to make a living in the Congo.

Mac repeated his question. "So what are you doing here this early?"

"A little business with Gabriel. Which I wanted to get over and done before the heat of the day."

Mac took off his wide-brimmed hat and wiped his forehead with a none too clean handkerchief. "I never knew you to get down to business so early." His icy blue eyes were speculative.

Alex managed an easy laugh. "You don't know all my habits, Mac. Believe it or not, I'd stay and explain them to you, but I'm in a hurry."

Mac wasn't ready to end the conversation. He walked along beside Alex. "I hear you've got a hotel full of guests. Any of them interested in a tour? The usual, you know, crocs, hippos. Maybe a visit to a quaint native village."

"Their time is all scheduled," Alex lied. He didn't want the guide involved in any of the events at Porte Ivoire—and certainly not in what happened yesterday, neither the murder nor the arrest. But news traveled fast in the jungle, and within another day, possibly another hour, everything would be known. He had to get out of here—and fast—there was no time for explanation to the Irish guide.

"See you around, pal."

Alex started on his way, Mac's voice trailing after him. "I might drive over anyway. Check it out. Maybe drum up a little business."

Alex kept walking, his lips closed in a hard line as he considered a possible predicament. Mac McQuire, despite his occasional drunken spree, was one of the best trackers in the Congo. Damned if he wanted the man on his trail. But what could he do?

Alex hesitated for a minute and looked back. There was a way to silence Mac, and he considered it briefly. An hour earlier, it might have been possible, but now the place was coming alive, and there were too many witnesses. His only choice was to trust Lady Luck and get the hell upriver.

"Here," Alex said gruffly to Dana. "My friend opened this coconut for you."

She took the coconut from him eagerly.

"And his wife sent freshly baked bread and fruit."

Dana was attempting to drink from the coconut without much success. "I guess there're no straws."

"Darn," Alex said with a sarcastic laugh. "I forgot to add them to our supplies. You'll just have to make do."

Shooting him a withering look, she turned the coconut upside down, attempting to get a few sips of milk, half of which dribbled down her chin. Alex refrained from comment as he pulled off a hunk of bread for her. "Here, try this. The combination is great." He swung into the Jeep. "I'll crack open the coconut and cut off some meat for you when we get to the boat."

"Where is it?" Dana asked as she chomped down on the soft, still-warm bread.

"A few miles upriver. We'll hide the Jeep by the bank and Gabriel will pick it up later."

"Can he be trusted?"

Alex shrugged as he maneuvered the Jeep onto the road. "As much as anyone. Better than most. He worked for me at the hotel for a while until he decided to come back here to his village to teach."

"There's a school here?" Dana couldn't mask her disbelief. "It's so remote."

"Doesn't matter. Schools in the Congo are commonplace. The children here are always eager to learn, and the literacy rate is eighty-five percent, something our own countries could aspire to."

"Sorry. I shouldn't judge by appearances. I'm sure your friend is a good person and won't tell Kantana about us," she said.

"But you're not convinced? Well, I can vouch for him. He'll pick up the Jeep when the heat is off, as the Americans say. Then the vehicle is his. It's a good trade. A boat to get us out of here for a Jeep that's worth nothing to us. Considering our situation," he added wryly.

As they bounced along the road, Alex made another dour comment. "There could be a problem, though."

"What?" She felt her heart sink. Didn't they have worries enough?

"You."

She bristled. "What now?"

"Can you paddle a canoe?"

She smiled and tried not to look too superior. "As a matter of fact, I've been canoeing since I was five. My two older brothers taught me everything about water sports—kayaking, white-water rafting—I can do it all because I learned from experts," she said smugly.

"Those were sports, as you say. This will be different."

"I can hold my own." Dana raised her chin defensively as she answered. "You don't have to worry about me."

"C'est bon," he told her. "Good. I don't intend to."

HOURS LATER—Dana wasn't sure how many; it seemed like an eternity—she regretted bragging. Her ideas of prowess in a canoe didn't include anything like this.

"This isn't a canoe!" was her first comment. As they got it out on the river, she saw how right she'd been. A hollowed-out log, it rode low in the water and was hard as hell to steer. It was nothing like the light fiberglass canoes she'd used in Colorado. A challenge, Alex had called out as he'd settled her in the bow and packed their supplies and tents around her.

The Lomami River was another challenge. It appeared sluggish and slow-moving, but the current was deceptive, Dana realized quickly, as it swirled unpredictably around them. Fighting off the current took all of her strength as well as her total concentration, and it immediately took its toll. After only a few miles of steady, hard paddling, sharp pains began to shoot across her shoulders and down her arms. Her palms were already blistered and raw from grasping the rough paddle. Now and then she stole a glance at the impenetrable green walls of vegetation along the banks. But this was no tour, and she wasn't a tourist; she was a fugitive. Even a short break in concentration could mean disaster.

To Alex's credit, she admitted grudgingly, he didn't criticize her. He didn't complain about her problems of adjusting to the canoe or the river. He gave her the benefit of the doubt and then let her prove herself. Which she did quickly. Only now and then did he have to call out for her to back paddle to avoid an impending sandbar—and there were plenty of those, insidious, snaky spits of land that appeared out of nowhere—or a tree limb lurking just beneath the surface, or a floating log that seemed to take deadly aim for the canoe.

She managed to pass all the tests. Even the crocodiles, although there was a moment when she almost lost it over the scaly reptiles. The first one she saw looked just like a log—until it opened its mouth in a wide yawn to reveal rows of huge, sharp teeth. She let out a yell and doubled her paddling speed.

The croc turned away disinterestedly, and as they sped by Dana tried not to think about what would have happened if the canoe had overturned, tried not to think about thrashing tails and slashing teeth. She focused only on the rhythm of her paddle cutting through the water—again and again and again.

The sun sank lower behind the trees as they moved on, sending golden shards of light across the river. By this time, Dana was barely aware of the primitive beauty of the scene. No longer an avid sightseer, she was consumed not by the scene but by the pain. Her shoulders ached and her hands were almost numb as they grasped the paddle. She paddled in a trance, barely noticing when the river widened into a brown, muddy pool. She was driven by the need to keep moving. And Alex's urging.

All she wanted was to get to a stopping place, to rest at last. She didn't believe anything could attract her attention. Then she saw something move near the bank. She cringed, expecting to see a scaly croc snout, wondering if she could speed up her paddling again. Then wide nostrils appeared, dark protruding eyes, round ears. She skipped a beat in her paddling and watched, mesmerized by the enormous, slow-moving creature.

"Hippos," she called out. "Look, Alex! There're hippos feeding." She was suddenly a tourist again, and she wanted to get closer. "This is fantastic," she said as she began to back paddle.

"Head for the opposite bank," Alex ordered.

She turned toward him. "No, I want to see the hippos—"

"Don't argue with me, Dana. Just paddle."

"But people don't see this kind of thing outside a zoo, and we're so close. They're not dangerous like crocs—"

"Do as I say." Alex was shouting now. "Those cows have calves, and they're protective as hell."

Just then more hippos materialized from under the muddy water. Less fascinating now, they seemed gigantic to Dana, powerful and awesome. Their sudden roars filled the air, and their great mouths opened, as cavernous as horrible, fleshy dungeons. They shook their heads from side to side, spewing river water in great shining arcs that glistened eerily in the sun.

Dana needed no further urging. She dug her paddle into the water, finding renewed strength as she kept in rhythm with Alex and headed toward the sandbar where a dead tree had lodged. It could provide a screen between them and the feeding hippos.

But Dana's hesitation had cost precious time, enough for one of the four-ton cows to come bellowing angrily through the water toward them. The hippo's roar was deafening, the power of her body terrifying. Huge waves rocked the canoe in her wake. While Dana and Alex fought to hold steady, the waves hit them broadside, splashing into the shallow boat. For a moment Dana was sure they would swamp, but she kept paddling even as the muscles in her shoulders and arms screamed out in pain, even as the huge beast closed in on them.

Then they reached the fallen tree and slipped the canoe into a narrow channel between it and the sandbar. The cow's way was blocked, and she bellowed once more in warning, impotently, and then turned and lumbered back toward her calves, now on the opposite bank.

Dana relaxed but only until Alex yelled out more orders to her. "Keep on paddling. We want to get as far out of their range as possible."

The hippos thrashed in the water and roared out their territorial rights, but there were no more charges. Alex and Dana guided the canoe around one bend and then another with the sounds of the animals fading in the distance.

Finally, she dropped the paddle in the boat, relaxed her tense shoulder and let out a deep shaky breath of relief. "I had no idea that hippos were so dangerous."

"They didn't look it at first, did they? Appearances again, eh, Dana? Just because they seem harmless in a zoo doesn't mean they are. A hippo can make splinters out of small boats. They're as deadly as crocs."

Dana shivered under the bright sun. Nothing in Africa was harmless, she decided. Danger was all around, lurking in wait for the uninitiated tourist. Well, she was a tourist no longer. A traveler, not a sightseer.

"Pick up the paddle again," Alex advised after a moment. "We still have a long way to go."

Dana nodded, but she'd lost her concentration. She was tired. No, not tired, exhausted. She couldn't lift the paddle one more time; she couldn't even think. She shut her eyes, only for a moment, hoping to regain her momentum. But it was no good. She was finished for the day, and if Alex had any compassion at all, he would let her stop.

"Alex—" That was all she got out as a sudden jolt shook the boat. Her lapse of concentration caused them to collide with a heavy log. The impact sent them spinning toward the bank, and when she leaned over to steady the boat with her paddle, the center of gravity suddenly shifted. Water taken on in the hippo attack sloshed to her side, and Dana slipped over, tipping the canoe with her. She didn't even have time to call out as she found herself sliding into the Lomami River, followed by Alex and a canoe full of supplies.

Chapter Five

Dana felt the river rush over her. She gasped, held her breath and struggled frantically for air. Overhead, she could see light through the murky water. She fought to get there, to breathe again.

Finally, she broke the surface, inhaled deeply and looked around, her mind filled with images. Hippos with gaping mouths. Crocodiles with slashing teeth. She'd seen them before, fought to flee them. Now she was in the water where they lived. She was in their territory, and her only desire was to get away, get to dry land.

She began to swim through the thick tepid water, grimy and filled with weeds. The shore wasn't that far away. She could make it. Then she saw Alex. He'd managed to grab the canoe, hold on and keep it from drifting away.

"Dana," he called out. "Help me right the canoe."

Still frantic to get out of the water and onto the shore, she forced herself to swim toward him instead.

"Get on this side," he ordered, "and we can turn it over easily." She did as she was told, and with their combined weight, the boat was upright. Luckily, most of their plastic-wrapped supplies were still lashed inside.

"Good job," he said. She had managed to stay afloat, even though exhaustion was closing in on her. "Collect the rest of the supplies, and I'll tow the canoe to shore."

Bundles wrapped in plastic floated all around them, and Dana realized that this time she wasn't going to obey his command. "No way," she said adamantly. "I'm not risking another minute in this slimy river waiting to be eaten by a croc or a hippo. I'll tow the boat, get it ashore and unload. *You* go after the supplies."

Just a few feet from him, frantically treading water, she watched in amazement as he began to laugh. She would never understand him. Never.

"Alex—"

"Go ahead, tow it," he said as he shook his head, flipped away the water and swam after the rest of their supplies.

Left to prove herself, Dana reached for the rope on the bow of the canoe, grabbed hold and began to swim with one-armed strokes, awkwardly pulling the canoe behind her. Finally she reached the shore, and as her feet found the bottom, she dragged the little boat behind her. Sinking deep into the mud, she slowly crawled ashore.

For a long moment she lay collapsed on the bank, still holding tightly to the rope. Finally she struggled to her feet and wrapped the rope around the trunk of a rotted tree. Once the canoe was secured, she looked out to the river and saw Alex swimming after the other supplies. Even though she really wanted to crawl into a safe place and sleep, Dana knew she had to do her part. She was responsible for the accident; the least she could do now was to complete her assignment.

She began to unload, pulling out the contents, unwrapping the plastic coverings and spreading everything out on the bank to dry under the hot sun. Among the supplies was her backpack, including her father's notes and her tape recorder. Alex had insisted she wrap the pack under her seat in the canoe. He'd been right, she admitted as she removed the tape recorder, clicked it on and found to her relief that the battery was still working. She might be able to record some of the Mgembe language—if they found the Pygmies. If they weren't captured first. And if they could stay alive....

After she finished unloading, Dana looked out at the river, expecting to see Alex's dark head bobbing along in the river.

He wasn't there. He seemed to have vanished around a bend in the river. Her heart caught in her throat. She didn't trust him, but she needed him, and she didn't want him to die—or to escape alone, if that was his agenda.

Dana rushed to the edge of the river and peered downstream. No Alex. She waded a few steps farther out, trying not to think about the dangers to herself, worrying instead about him. What could have happened? Suddenly she found herself alone—and afraid. She waded even farther. Nothing mattered now, not when she was faced with the possibility of being stranded—alone in an unfamiliar jungle.

"Alex!" she called out.

"Missing me already, Dana?"

She swirled around and saw him coming toward her, striding along the riverbank, carrying their supplies over his shoulder.

"I was a little concerned," she admitted, adding, "because I need you in order to survive. Like it or not."

Alex dropped everything onto the bank. "And the need is mutual—like it or not."

Dana tried not to stare at him, but she couldn't tear her eyes away. He stood before her, water dripping from his hair, his chin and down his clothes. His shirt and pants were molded to his body, which only emphasized the muscles of his chest and legs.

Even wet, he had an undeniable power. It was both physical and emotional, and it was impossible to ignore. Especially here on the desolate riverbank. And since she was the one responsible for putting them in the middle of this situation, Dana said what was on her mind. "I'm sorry. About tipping over the canoe. It was a stupid mistake. I guess the hippos unnerved me."

"Forget it," he said tersely. "It happened. I'm not thrilled about it, but we can deal with the problems. The canoe came through in one piece. I managed to round up almost all the food and supplies."

"Almost?"

"Lost one tent. That's all."

She sighed. It wasn't so terrible after all. "You're not angry?" she asked.

He shrugged. "Sure I am, but that doesn't help the situation, does it?" He walked to the edge of the river and looked upstream. "I don't think we can get any farther today, even though I'd like to."

Dana didn't tell him that she couldn't paddle another yard, much less another mile, whether he'd like to or not.

"So we'll make camp, dry off and fix something for dinner."

Dry clothes, food—and then sleep. The combination sounded heavenly to Dana.

Alex handed her a nylon duffel bag. "I expect the clothes in here are dry."

"Thanks." She untied it and pulled out a pair of shorts and a shirt. "Dry as a bone." As she stood up, she found that he had already begun to undress. She watched openmouthed as he stripped off his shirt, draped it over a tree limb to dry and turned toward her, a half smile on his face.

Seeing him almost naked was just too much. His upper torso was sleek and tanned with well-delineated muscles and broad shoulders. A dusting of dark hair began on his chest and tapered downward toward his belly button. Her eyes stayed there, even though she willed them to move upward.

He caught her glance—and made the most of it, reaching for the zipper of his pants.

Dana backed up a step. "I'll change somewhere—" She looked around. "Somewhere else." With that she turned quickly and headed for a tall screen of bushes.

"You don't have to run away, Dana," he called after her. "We can both change here. I'm not a prude—"

He was right about that, she thought as she trudged on.

"All right," he said. "But don't forget—"

She stopped. "What?"

"When you change your socks, be sure and put your shoes back on. There're lots of snakes around."

She stopped short, peering warily into the thick green vegetation. "Poisonous?"

"About half of them, I imagine, but it probably wouldn't be a good idea to find out which—"

"Don't worry," Dana said as she looked anxiously around. "I'm getting dressed quickly. I hope you'll do the same." She began to unbutton her blouse. Now it had begun, she and Alex alone together in the vastness of the rain forest.

Just then a troop of monkeys swept by in the trees overhead, screaming out their irritation of the strangers' intrusion. Dana smiled and pulled off her soaked blouse. Alone, but not totally.

THE FIRE flickered brightly in the black night. They'd made camp, talking only when necessary, and eaten dinner, a meal part fresh but mostly packaged.

After they finished, Alex cleaned up while Dana, giving in to her exhaustion, stretched out and watched night fall over the river, a swift, impenetrable darkness that descended like a curtain once the sun was down.

She closed her eyes—just for a moment—and when she opened them, Alex had put up one of their tents. She looked around for the other one and remembered what had happened. They'd lost a tent to the river. At first she hadn't realized what that meant. Now it was suddenly very clear to her. Tonight—and all of the nights to come—would have to be spent together in a single dwelling.

She was wary but in a way also relieved to know that they would be close together during the black jungle nights. Right now he and the fire were her only protection. A few feet away the jungle threatened, its sounds magnified in the black night. She moved a little closer as strange calls echoed through the trees and unknown rustlings moved the bushes. Each unfamiliar sound made the hairs along her neck rise and her imagination run wild.

"Snakes and what else in the bush?" she asked uneasily.

"Leopard. Water buffalo. Elephant. But they're as afraid of you as you are of them. They'll stay out of our way. I've always said that the most dangerous predator in the Congo is man."

"Kantana, you mean." Again, she felt the need to move closer to Alex. "He'll be after us soon, won't he?"

Alex shrugged. "Probably. There's nothing we can do about that now. Except keep going. Stay a step ahead."

She looked at his profile in the flickering firelight. Shadows played along the strong planes of his face. He looked handsome—and a little sinister. There was a golden glow about him that was terribly appealing as well as a hardness that made her uncomfortable and wary.

"Do you ever have regrets, about anything?"

"I try not to. It serves no purpose," he answered easily.

"No regrets about leaving the hotel?"

His laugh was sardonic. "None. I won the damned place in a card game so I don't have much invested in it."

"In a card game?" she repeated.

"It's a long story," he equivocated.

"Tell me. After all, we have lots of time, the whole night ahead of us." Dana knew she was avoiding spending the night in their shared tent, and for good reason. She had shared a small space with him only once before—the closet at the Stanley Hotel. That episode burned in her memory. She and Alex had been pressed against each other, their bodies almost entwined, and her emotions had almost gotten out of hand. She didn't want to take a chance like that again. So she preferred to stay here, close to him, but in the open next to the fire.

"I guess that's true. We can't go anywhere in the dark of night." He shifted slightly and settled back against a tree. "I never planned to end up in Porte Ivoire. I followed someone there. A woman."

She wasn't surprised. "A tourist?"

"No, she was a doctor. I was in North Africa working in import-export when I met Giselle. She had a strong desire to heal the whole world. You've probably heard of *Médecins sans Frontières*—Doctors Without Borders. Giselle was sent through the organization to train medical assistants for Father Theroux's mission in Porte Ivoire. At about that time, it was suggested that I remove myself from Tunis."

"The police threw you out?" Here she was again, Dana thought, face-to-face with more about his unsavory activities.

"The authorities weren't pleased with what I was importing—or exporting. So I decided to tag along with Giselle."

"Were you in love with her?" She was surprised by the bluntness of her question.

Alex chuckled. "You're awfully nosy, Dana."

"I didn't mean—" Just then a scream reverberated through the jungle, and she moved instinctively closer to him.

"Who is it?" she cried.

Alex laughed. "Not who, but what. A night bird."

"Bird!" Dana couldn't believe it.

"They're noisy creatures," he said. "So are monkeys. Hyenas. You name it. The animals of night are a rambunctious bunch. So relax and adapt, Dana. This is just the beginning."

She tried to take his advice, moving away from him, but not too far away, and getting back to the conversation. "About Giselle—"

"I suppose we were in lust, not love. We were both too self-centered to fall in love, but things were great at first. She worked at Theroux's clinic, I took over the hotel. We met at night in bed."

She looked at him in the firelight and saw a smile creep across his face. "I usually don't talk about myself."

"I'd like to hear the end of the story," she insisted.

"Why not? I've gone this far." He settled against the tree comfortably. "Giselle completed her assignment and was ready to move on. But I was just getting the Stanley operable again. Tourists were stopping for the day and deciding to stay overnight. The hotel business was beginning to seem like a lot of fun. So she went, and I stayed."

"And you have no regrets." It was a statement rather than a question.

"Not a one. She's happy, I guess. As for myself, I had a good time for a while, and now I'm on my way out of the Congo."

"On your very secret mission," Dana continued, unable to keep the sarcasm out of her voice.

"You sound skeptical."

"Maybe just a little doubtful," she admitted.

"That's your prerogative, Dana."

"Well, since I'm involved in this scheme, don't you think I should know more about it?"

"Knowing more could put your life in danger."

"Like I'm not in danger now?" She was incredulous. "I'm in this thing up to my armpits, so I'd like to know more about those so-called secret documents."

"An adamant woman," Alex said with a sigh as he stared into the darkness. He could see the faint gleam of the Lomami River in the moonlight and the silhouette of giant trees against the sky. The setting was dramatic and beautiful; so was the woman. The firelight drew them together in an intimate circle of warmth— and all she wanted to do was interrogate him.

Well, that wasn't going to happen, Alex decided. Talking to her about Giselle was harmless. But there'd be no discussion of Louis or his particular mission or the circumstances that led to his death. That would be treading on dangerous ground. He wasn't going to indulge her.

"So I'm adamant," she admitted. "Does that mean you're going to tell me about the documents or not?" she persisted.

"I'll tell you. In time," he added. "I swear that you'll know everything you have to know."

Her silence told him that she wasn't satisfied; in fact, she didn't believe him. Too bad. There was nothing he could do about that. Except get her off the subject of the damned "mission." Alex smiled to himself. That wouldn't be difficult, considering her state of mind about the jungle. She'd even nestled close to him when the birds called out. Now she was only inches away. The isolation of the jungle would work in his favor. She had no one but him.

Still, Alex determined to go slowly, not alarm her. He ran his fingers along her shoulder, and when she didn't move away, he leaned forward and touched the delicate ivory carving she wore around her neck. Beneath his fingers, against the warmth of her throat, he could feel her racing pulse.

Her eyes held his for a long moment; there was wariness in them . . . and something else. He'd felt it when they were pressed together in the closet. And he felt it now. Could it be attraction? Excitement? There was no denying the spark that flickered between them, and time was on his side.

"I hadn't noticed the necklace," he said softly.

She shrugged, which allowed her to move away again. Alex withdrew his hand, reminding himself to go slow and easy. He needed her trust . . . and her help. "Were you wearing it before?"

"No," she admitted, wrapping her fingers around the talisman. "After the canoe capsized, I was relieved that it hadn't been lost, so I decided to wear it from now on. My father gave me the necklace, and it means a lot to me. It comes from the Mgembe," she added.

"The Pygmies?" Alex's surprise was apparent.

"Yes, they carved the talisman and gave it to my father as a sign of friendship."

"Incredible," he said, his lips curving in a pleased smile. "But very lucky for us." The Lady had smiled one more time on her favorite son, he realized. "We need any edge we can get with the Pygmies."

"*If* we find them."

"Oh, we'll find them—unless they find us first." Alex expected that the moment they reached Mgembe territory, the Pygmies would know they were there. But he didn't know whether they'd be friendly or hostile. That's where Dana came in.

In case things didn't go well, he needed to keep her on his side—and by his side. They needed to think alike, move in unison, act as a perfect team. But how to accomplish that? She wasn't like Giselle or Betty, eager for sexual adventure with a stranger. She had all kinds of defenses that would have to be broken down. Slowly, carefully.

"Do you think that—"

Alex raised his hand in a motion of protest. "No more, Dana. It's my turn to ask the questions."

"What can I possibly tell you?"

"The truth about yourself."

She laughed. "You've heard everything about me. Why I came here...my teaching job in Colorado and my father's background with the Mgembe. I *used* to lead a perfectly normal life," she said, almost bitterly. "I was a very normal person, a teacher. My only adventures took place on the pages of books."

Alex sat quietly, letting her go on, listening.

"Nothing prepared me for being arrested for murder and trekking through the rain forest and getting pursued by maddened hippos—" She looked up, saw his grin and broke off.

"There must have been some excitement in your life. Some romance. What about boyfriends, lovers? Maybe a white knight from America who will come charging to your rescue in the jungle?"

"Only my brothers—if Millie ever gets through to them."

"Only your brothers? I can't believe that. You're much too beautiful not to have a cadre of men panting after you."

"Panting! I'm afraid not, Alex."

"No lovers at all?"

"No. Not now." She raised her chin defensively, a look he was beginning to recognize. "But there was—"

She broke off and he waited silently.

"I was engaged in college."

"What happened?" he asked bluntly, causing her to bristle.

"Nothing *happened*." She shook her head as if to rid herself of his questions. "I can't imagine why I'm discussing this with you."

"Because I told you about Giselle, because we're together here, alone in the jungle, and it's time we got to know each other. But mostly because I'm curious. There's nothing wrong with telling me about your life, your loves." He ventured to touch her again, in a friendly way, on the arm. "Do you think you'll shock me?" he teased.

"You?" She cocked an eyebrow. "That would be impossible! And I don't suppose there's anything wrong with my telling you about my life and loves. But there was only one love: His name was Roger."

"And?"

She gave in. "Okay. We were engaged during my senior year. We planned to marry after graduation, but put it off. Roger went to grad school in New York State, and I got a fellowship at the University of Colorado. We soon found that long-distance relationships don't work."

"I guess you're the kind of woman who likes closeness. Being together. Sharing everything."

Dana thought she heard condescension in his voice and she reacted defensively. "Yes, I do, and there's nothing wrong with that."

"Of course not," he agreed. "I'm all for it. We have it going right here. Closeness. Being together—"

"It's not the same," she protested, her eyes wary again.

"I was joking, Dana."

"I know that." Some of the tension left her face, and her expression softened.

Alex steered the conversation back to her. "I'll bet neither you nor your boyfriend wanted to compromise."

"No, we didn't. Besides, I had my goals. Important ones," she added.

"I'm sure you did," he said, with as much understanding as possible.

But she still looked sharply at him. Alex kept his face expressionless. A picture of Dana was coming together for him. Bright. Hardworking. Goal-oriented. And also stubborn and inquisitive. A little touchy, but what the hell? She was the kind of woman he liked, the kind who would make a perfect partner on their journey because her attributes could be translated into good survival skills. Maybe they would balance each other and make it to safety. If he handled her correctly.

He leaned closer so that their shoulders touched. By turning his head slightly, he could catch a glimpse of her as she looked away from him, out into the night. The sweep of her lashes. Her finely etched nose. And her mouth. Sweet, generous, sensual.

"Come on," he urged, "tell me more about yourself." He spoke easily, casually, all the while thinking about her mouth. About kissing her. That had been on his mind since the first time he'd seen her.

"Well, I became a teacher, like my father," she offered.

"So his advice was important in your career decision?"

"Yes," she replied, "but I'll never be as brilliant as he was."

"What about his other opinions? Did he approve of Roger, who wanted to take you away from the world of ancient languages?"

"My parents both died before I finished college," she answered.

"Sorry. I didn't know." He waited a moment before continuing. "Did your big brothers like Roger?"

Dana shrugged.

"That means no, doesn't it? I bet no one is good enough for little sister."

Dana shot him a nasty look. "That's not true. If my brothers are a little protective, it's because they have my best interests at heart. They did point out the advantages of staying in Colorado where my family is known, and they were right. It certainly worked for them. Andy is a successful city planner and Kurt's a brilliant lawyer. If he'd been in Porte Ivoire, things would have turned out differently."

Alex chuckled at her impassioned defense. "I'd hate to be the man who tried to get past your brothers to get to you."

"You'll never have to worry about that," she snapped. "And anyway, I live my own life."

She was getting angry, and Alex was sorry he'd pushed the questions about her brothers. She was touchy about their protectiveness, but he couldn't help liking the passionate way she defended them even though it made him strangely jealous.

"I apologize for being nosy," he said quickly, easily. "Your family life is none of my business." Things had been going so well, he didn't want to antagonize her now.

"You're right about that," she said coolly. Dana picked up a stick and poked at the dwindling embers.

Alex let out a low whistle. "*Mon Dieu*—your hands. They're blistered."

Dana drew her hands back quickly. "They're not that bad."

"Let me see," he ordered.

"That's not necessary." She tucked her hands behind her back for a moment before realizing that she had no reason to be ashamed of blisters. Especially since they were caused by his insistence that they keep on paddling in spite of her exhaustion! She held out her hands.

Alex took them in his. The blisters had broken open and were oozing and painful. "I'll take care of these," he said. She was about to change her view of Alex and conclude that there could be a trace of kindness in him, after all, when he added, "Otherwise, you'll be no good for paddling tomorrow."

"We certainly can't have that," she said sarcastically.

He still held her hands, but his voice softened. "I don't mean to make light of the pain you're feeling, Dana. I'll try to take care of that. But we have to move on. That's most important. We both need to be in good shape. Agreed?"

"Agreed," she said, somewhat chastised.

Alex got up and rummaged in his knapsack until he found the salve. "Give me your hands."

She hesitated a moment.

"Try to think of me less as the big bad wolf and more as a healer." He knelt in front of her, and she held out her hands.

Even though his touch was gentle, his fingers gliding softly across her abused palms, Dana decided he was more wolf than healer. His face was only inches from hers and she could study every line and nuance. His dark lashes couldn't hide the green fire of his eyes, and his strongly shaped lips were sensual in their masculinity. Firelight flickered provocatively along the planes of his cheekbones. She felt an unexpected prickle of tension skitter along her spine at the pressure of his fingers. Was it anxiety or anticipation?

He continued to work on her hands, smoothing the salve along her palms and down her fingers. His motions were caressing, sensuous; heat radiated from his fingers and rippled along her skin. She thought of asking him to stop, but she knew he wouldn't. There was danger in being so close to him, but there was also pleasure... and need. His fingers were long and lean, and she wondered what it would be like if he touched her in other places, intimate, sensitive areas. Dana gave a little shiver as the fantasy played out in her head.

Alex, carefully rubbing the salve, glanced at her. She'd caught her bottom lip between her teeth and closed her eyes. He'd felt her shiver, wondered if he'd hurt her, but instinct told him something else was going on. A tension emanated from her that was almost palpable. He smiled and ran his fingers along her palms. Her very kissable lips gave out a little sigh.

Her mouth was close, so close.... And he was going to kiss her. Not in the moonlight of the Stanley Hotel's garden or in the cloying dark of the closet, but here, now, in the hot African night, with firelight flickering and the moon above.

She opened her eyes and smiled at him, withdrawing her hands. "Thanks."

He realized it was the first genuine smile she'd given him.

"My hands feel better already." She lightly rubbed them together.

He didn't move from his place in front of her. "So I'm a good medicine man."

She nodded.

"And not a wolf?" He raised a dark eyebrow.

"That's still up for debate." Her laugh was nervous, but her eyes met his directly.

"Okay, I'm something of a wolf, but only around a beautiful..." There was no way he could stop himself. He leaned forward, and his lips grazed hers. "Desirable woman..."

It was meant to be a light, teasing kiss, but when he tasted her lips, everything changed. He realized how much he wanted her—and wanted her to want *him*. She tried to turn her head, but he wouldn't let her. He tilted her face toward him, held her chin firmly with his hand and kissed her.

Her mouth opened softly under his, and he tasted her fully. Their tongues touched, slick, hot, and he felt her shiver, strain toward him, slide her arms around his neck. Alex drew her closer, heard her tremulous sigh, felt her breasts firm and full, pressing against him. His blood pounded with need and longing. He wanted to discover more of her. So much more...

Dana felt herself melting against him, giving herself to the kiss and to his taste and touch. His tongue skated across her teeth, probed the deep recesses of her mouth, thrust, withdrew. His mouth moved upon hers, hungry, seeking, and she kissed him back eagerly, taking his tongue in her mouth, mating it with hers, drinking in his kisses.

She felt suspended, awash with sensation. She knew she should pull away, stop the madness of the kiss, but how could she? Her body betrayed her with each breath. Her nipples tingled, swelled. A warm sweetness swept over her, and she could feel that same warmth between her legs, hotter, becoming a flame of tension and excitement as it built dangerously fast.

She was losing control as she became caught up completely in the kiss, the feel of his arms, the taste of his lips and the dizziness of desire. She felt his hand slide between their bodies, cup her breast. She was open to him, vulnerable. His fingers brushed her aching nipple, fumbled for the button on her shirt. Was this what she wanted? She didn't know. His demanding lips left hers for an instant, and in that moment she struggled for an answer and fought for control.

With a little moan, Dana tore her mouth from his and struggled to her feet, legs shaky and uncertain. She'd been vulnerable, but she didn't want to admit to herself how much; she certainly didn't want him to know how much. "Not a good idea," she managed to blurt through ragged breath.

Alex stood up beside her. "Seemed like a great idea to me. And admit it, Dana, you enjoyed it, too." He was breathing as hard as she, and his voice was edged with need.

"Blame it on the circumstances," she said. "We've been thrown together in an intimate situation, and so, naturally—" Her voice was as shaky as her legs.

"Naturally," he repeated. "But it's more than the circumstances."

He ran his fingers lightly along her cheek. Her skin tingled under his touch. He held her chin in his hand, his green eyes locked on hers. His gaze was hypnotic, drawing her toward him. It mesmerized her. If he pulled her close, tried to kiss her again—

She had to break the spell, to distance herself. She managed to take one step backward, and that was enough. He dropped his hand, but he held her with his voice and with his seductive words.

"Admit it, Dana. You secretly crave excitement, adventure, the unknown. That's why you're really here in the Congo, away from school, Colorado, your brothers. It may even be why you're here in my arms."

"I'm not in your arms," she shot back.

"That can be easily remedied. Reach out for what you want, Dana. Reach out and try it."

She looked into his green, unfathomable eyes. It was easy to be drawn toward him, to be pulled by his sensual power. But she wasn't going to be seduced. "No," she said sharply. "There're too many complications for us to make love."

"Make love?" He grinned at her. "Is that what you thought I meant?" He feigned a look of surprise. "And all this time, I thought we were just sharing a friendly kiss. I didn't know—"

"Damn you, Alex." She turned and stalked away from him—and his cocky smile and teasing words—stopping in front of the bright orange tent. "Only one tent for us to share," she said angrily. "You probably let the other one float away on purpose."

"Let me remind you who was responsible for overturning the canoe, Dana."

There was no winning with this man, she thought as she pulled open the flap and stepped into the tent. She could have suggested he sleep outside, but she knew that wouldn't wash, and she wasn't about to leave herself open to more abuse from him. The only choice was to get to sleep quickly, before he followed her into the tent.

Dana checked her sleeping bag for scorpions, snakes and spiders. Then she took off her shoes and zipped herself in. She lay there, tense, listening to Alex move around outside, trying to will herself to sleep.

But she was still wide awake when he came into the tent and crawled into his sleeping bag beside her.

"I'd rather you sleep outside the tent," she said tersely.

"*Ma chérie*," he said softly, "*voulez-vous coucher avec moi ce soir?*"

Dana understood the suggestive French phrase, *do you want to go to bed with me tonight?*

"No!" she said adamantly.

"Ah, so you speak French," Alex said.

"I'm a linguist, remember? But it certainly doesn't take one to translate that."

"Well, don't worry," he said softly. "I won't accost you in your sleeping bag. You know why?" He smiled and answered his own question. "Because it wouldn't be any fun. Remember, I only want to make love when you want to." After a beat he added, "And I know you want to."

Slapping him would be pointless—and hell on her already painful hands. Any other kind of response would be equally pointless against his cleverness. She opted for silence.

Then, in the dark night, came a loud coughing noise. Dana sat up like a shot. It sounded human. Could it possibly be Kantana so soon? "Who is it?" she asked Alex.

His voice was sleepy. "Not who, Dana. Last time it was a bird, now it's a leopard."

Leopard! It sounded so close, only yards away. "Alex?"

"Yes?"

"Do you have a gun?" she asked.

"Yes."

"Do you know how to use it?"

"Of course."

She smiled in the darkness. "Good."

THE SHADOWS OF DEATH loomed closer and closer. Louis was dead and buried, his bones forever resting in Africa, not the ending he would have wanted, but so much of life depended on chance and opportunity.

His death was unfortunate but necessary. In the end, I knew he wouldn't simply hand over his prize. He would protect what he had stolen. But would he, too, have killed for it?

The answer came softly on the night air, like the moaning of a cypress as it bent with the wind.

Chapter Six

"*Bon matin*, Dana."

The voice was soft and caressing against her earlobe.

But Dana wasn't interested in lulling tones. She was still exhausted; she needed more than one night's sleep to make up for what she'd missed. She closed her eyes tightly and scrunched lower into her sleeping bag.

"Get up, Dana. The sun got up half an hour ago. Time for you to do the same."

She groaned and cuddled into a ball. "Just a little while longer," she begged.

"No." His voice was more insistent now. "It's not time to sleep; it's time to leave." He tugged at the sleeping bag, and a shaft of sunlight hit her in the face.

"Turn off the light!" she demanded.

Alex moved to the opening of the tent and held back the flap. "Five seconds and you're up—or I dump you in the river, sleeping bag and all."

"Okay, okay." Dana crawled out, pushed past Alex into the sun, grimacing under its brightness. She was sore and stiff; she ached in places where she never knew she had muscles. "I smell coffee," she said, beginning to wake up.

"But you don't get any—"

"What?"

"Until you get yourself together." He thrust a canteen of water and a towel at her. "I'll have the tent down in five minutes. You have the same amount of time to get ready. Then a quick cup of coffee, and we're back on the river."

She pushed her hair out of her face, rubbed her eyes and looked up at him. To Dana's surprise, he seemed tired, too. And worried. The teasing look had disappeared from his eyes, replaced by concern. Tense lines of anxiety outlined his mouth. He wore the same clothes he'd slept in, and they were as wrinkled and creased as her own.

Now wasn't the time to argue, she decided. "I'll hurry." She grabbed her toothbrush and cosmetic kit and headed to her private toilet behind the bushes. At the far end of the clearing, she'd created her own little bathroom the night before. After taking care of the needs of nature, she moved toward a semicircle of bushes where she quickly set up a dressing room. She pulled off her shorts and T-shirt, sloshed herself with water, toweled off and then put on the same wrinkled clothes. At least she was clean underneath.

She ran a brush through her matted hair, getting out the worst tangles, and tied it away from her face. After brushing her teeth, Dana applied a little blush and lipstick from her cosmetic kit, then laughed. Her hands were blistered, her hair was matted and dirty, her clothes were wrinkled and damp. And here she was, putting on makeup!

As she started toward camp, she rehearsed in her mind her speech to Alex. She was going to tell him calmly but firmly that theirs was a partnership. She was tired of being ordered around. He wasn't a marine sergeant; she wasn't a recruit, even if she had been recruited into this harebrained scheme.

Lost in thought, she was confused when she heard voices, or believed she did. Impossible, she decided, trudging on. Then she realized the voices weren't in her mind. Someone was at the camp with Alex. Instinctively, she dropped to her knees, crawled forward and peered through a tangle of vines. She saw the imposing figure of Jean Luc Kantana striding into camp.

His gun drawn, Kantana was accompanied by another man in uniform, who carried a rifle. Alex stood perfectly still near the ashes of the fire, his eyes on the two men.

Dana realized that she was shaking like a leaf. She tried to calm herself, but it was impossible. Her throat was so dry she could hardly swallow, and she was sure that the men could hear the pounding of her heart. This was the end. Soon the police would come after her and find her, drag her back to Porte Ivoire. Her jailbreak would convince Kantana of her guilt.

Dana held her breath. She could feel the perspiration pop out on her forehead as she listened to Kantana's angry voice.

Speaking in rapid French, he denounced Alex for masterminding the jailbreak of the American murderess, as he called Dana. In flowery rhetoric, Kantana berated Alex for letting him down, humiliating him. He'd been betrayed by a friend, and he planned retribution when they returned to Porte Ivoire. There, Alex would look forward to a very long jail sentence.

The long diatribe was followed by Alex's denial that she was with him. Kantana laughed at that.

"We have Victor's testimony that you overpowered him to break the American out of jail. I imagine she was your accomplice when Monsieur Longongo was attacked. The woman is with you now, my friend. I will find her and personally escort her—and you—back to jail.''

Dana felt her stomach rise into her throat. For a moment she thought she was going to be sick. But she held back the nausea. Now was the time to act. But how? She could flee into the rain forest alone, leaving Alex to his fate—and last about a day without food, supplies or a gun.

She buried her head in her hands. What could she do—rush Kantana, distract him, make a commotion? And then what? Dana heaved a sigh.

Maybe she should turn herself in, beg for mercy.

She looked through the vines and saw Kantana's face. Cold. Hard. Implacable. Totally without mercy. No, dammit, she wasn't going to give herself over to that policeman. Dana felt as though a cold icy hand had grasped her throat. She forced herself to breathe slowly, relax, think. If she couldn't give up, what could she do?

While she searched her mind for an answer, she heard Alex talking, asking about Victor, reacting to Kantana's arrogance easily. He was buying time for her. But for what? What did he expect her to do?

She closed her eyes and prayed for inspiration. She felt like a novice, here on the banks of the Lomami, but maybe she wasn't. Even though her hands were blistered from paddling, she was actually far from inexperienced; she knew how to handle a boat. She'd spent her childhood summers canoeing with her brothers in the Colorado mountains. They were experts, and she'd soaked up all their knowledge. ''My three water babies,'' her mother had called them.

Those skills might be the answer! Dana turned and began to crawl through the undergrowth toward the river.

What had seemed like an hour, while she'd watched Kantana and tried to formulate a plan, had been only a matter of minutes. They were still arguing—Kantana and Alex—as she made her way to the river, at first crawling and then, when her arm muscles began to shake from fear and tension, wriggling on her stomach, trying not to think of what else might be lurking in the jungle foliage.

She smelled the river before she saw it, ripe, fecund, fertile. There it was—no more than ten feet away. Cautiously, she peered over the tall grass and saw Kantana's boat, tied near the canoe. It was an old outboard, almost identical to the first one her brothers had owned when she was a child.

As she steeled herself for what she had to do, Dana heard something rustling in the bushes close to her. She held her breath, willing herself not to make a sound, determined not to scream. She remembered Alex's words. Animals were afraid of humans. They wouldn't bother her if she didn't bother them. She remained still and silent, frozen in the moment, waiting for the animal attack that never came.

Stifling a sob, she began to creep again, silently, through the grass. Alex had been right, she admitted. Then she heard another rustling, closer than before. She stopped again, waiting. She was frightened of what might be lurking there. But she was much more frightened of Kantana. She couldn't let him catch her; she couldn't go back to that jail. Ever.

Dana squirmed quickly to the riverbank and dropped over the edge into the water, never looking back. For a brief moment, she closed her eyes, waiting for whatever had been in the brush to dive in after her—or for the sharp teeth of a croc to clamp around her legs. Nothing happened. A few yards away, the water lapped indolently against the boat. Moving as silently as possible, she slid toward it, keeping the boat between her and the view from camp. She had a plan—of sorts—and it was time to put it into action.

She reached the boat and grabbed hold at the stern. The propeller was pulled up, out of the shallow water; the boat's bottom rested firmly on the mud. Cautiously, she looked over the side of the boat. It was amazing, she thought, how familiar it was, complete with the same wooden seats, plastic flotation cushions, paddles in case of emergency and the extra can of gasoline. The boat brought back many memories of long, lazy summers at the river. Kurt and Andy had started out with one similar to this and moved on to more sophisticated types. When she was old enough, Dana inherited the old motorboat.

And she learned everything about it. Including what made it go and what made it stop. Now was the time to make it stop. Without pausing to consider her decision, Dana inhaled deeply and dove underwater.

She snaked her hand along bottom of the boat near the propeller, searching for the gas line. The water was thick and murky. She couldn't see anything; all she could do was feel. She moved her hand backward and forward, expecting to find the rubbery plastic tube. Weeds wrapped around her as she flailed aimlessly. Her lungs about to burst, she kept searching, sure the line was close, within her reach.

Finally, unable to hold her breath any longer, she went up for air. Stupid, she told herself. Any idiot would be able to find the gas line within seconds, even in the muck and weeds. Now, when time was everything, she was wasting it. At this point, Kantana was probably ready to send his aide in search of her.

After a moment of mental hysteria, she got her act together, dove again and was immediately successful. Her hand felt the line, and her heart skipped a beat. Summoning all her energy, she grabbed hold and pulled downward.

It was done, but it wasn't enough. Eventually, Kantana and his aide might be able to repair the line, refill the tank and get underway again. She had to do more.

Crouching low in the water, she made her way to the bow and found the anchor rope, secured to a large rock. All she had to do was tug the rope loose and push the boat out into the current.

The rope slid silently into the water and bobbled on the surface before it sank. Dana leaned her weight against the boat and attempted to edge it toward the open water. It didn't budge. A couple of strong men could've moved it easily; she'd seen her brothers make the maneuver in a matter of seconds. She lacked the strength.

A sob rose in her throat. Even if a miracle occurred and she and Alex managed to overpower Kantana and his henchman, they'd be fools to leave the police with any means of pursuit. She *had* to move it. Turning around, she put her back and shoulders against the boat and braced her feet on the bank. She took a deep breath, counted to three and with every muscle straining, pushed.

Nothing. The muscles in her legs trembled from exertion; her heart pounded like an anvil. She wanted to scream in frustration and anger. Instead, she took another deep breath and pushed again, feeling the burn throughout her body. It paid off. There was slight movement. She tried again and felt the boat slowly inch away. She heard the scraping noise of wood against the muddy bottom of the river, and suddenly the motorboat was free, caught in the strong current of the Lomami. She guided it past the canoe toward the open water and with one final push watched it float away.

Quickly, she swam for cover in the grass by the bank and waited.

Only moments later she heard a voice crying out, *"Le bateau! Le bateau!"* Kantana's aide came charging toward the riverbank, waving his arms and shouting incoherently as the boat slid by. Kantana remained at the campsite, his gun still aimed at Alex. Under other circumstances, she would have found the situation overwhelmingly humorous—a portly policeman chasing a runaway boat, shouting curses at it in French. But she was too scared and tired to laugh. She had to worry about her next move.

Peering through the grass, she watched Kantana, who eyed Alex suspiciously. He must have known this wasn't an accident, but he was getting no affirmation from Alex, whose expression was innocent, almost bemused. She knew that the two men wouldn't be alone for long. As soon as the deputy discovered that their boat was irretrievable, he'd be back. It was now or never.

Dana understood what she had to do, but she didn't work out any details, make any plan. If she stopped to do that, even for a moment, it would be too late—and she would be paralyzed with fear. She moved instinctively.

As she charged through the grass toward them, she saw Alex's eyes widen in surprise. That look lasted less than a millisecond before his forehead creased, his lips tightened and his body tensed in preparation. In that instant, she knew he would do whatever it took to make her foolhardy attack work.

Kantana heard her coming and whirled toward the sound, his gun ready, aimed directly at her. It seemed to Dana as if she was moving in slow motion through a nightmare in which she ran and ran but made no progress. Her feet were mired in cement; she was going nowhere. Alex, too, seemed to move in slow motion, his body tensed, poised and then floating through the air toward Kantana.

The two men collided with a horrible thud. The sergeant tried to stay upright, but Alex grabbed his gun arm and wrestled him to the ground. As they rolled over, first one of them on top and then the other, Dana looked around frantically for a weapon of some kind. At the edge of the campsite she saw what was left of the wood they'd gathered for the fire. She grabbed the thickest piece and rushed toward the two fighting men, brandishing her makeshift club.

Now everything sped up, fast forwarding within her nightmare, out of control. Dana moved through it, frantically following the men as they rolled on the ground, grunting and cursing. She saw the glint of the gun, still in Kantana's hand. Alex had caught his arm at the wrist and held him like a vise, banging it against the ground, but Kantana wouldn't release the gun. His curses filled the air.

Dana raised her club and then, just as they rolled over again with Kantana on top, she closed her eyes and brought it down with all the force she possessed. It caught Kantana on the shoulder just inches from Alex's head. The sergeant screamed in pain and dropped the gun.

"Pick it up," Alex rasped as he rolled over on Kantana.

Stupefied by what she'd done, Dana stood, numb, looking at the two men. If her club had come down an inch or two on the other side, she would have knocked Alex out. She was panicked by the thought of that near catastrophe.

Then Alex's words came to her again through the fog of thought. "Dammit, Dana, get the gun."

She picked it up and held it in both hands, unsteadily. Shaking all over, she attempted to point the gun at Kantana.

"No!" Alex yelled. He had the policeman in a neck hold, arms locked behind his back. "Don't aim that thing or you'll kill us both. Just get his cuffs."

"What?" Dana stared at Alex.

"The handcuffs. They're on his belt. Hurry, Dana. I can't hold him forever."

Kantana continued to kick and struggle as she scrabbled to unhook the cuffs from his belt. Together, she and Alex handcuffed him, and then Dana sank to the ground, head in her hands, while Alex held the gun on Jean Luc Kantana.

"You're doing great," he praised her. "Just great. But don't fold on me now. We have to take care of Jean Luc's toady when he gets back. Then we'll get the hell out."

Kantana struggled to a seated position on the ground. He shook his head in an apparent daze. "It won't be that easy, Alex. Perhaps you get away this time, but I will follow." His eyes shifted to Dana. "And for the mademoiselle, if you come with us now, you may have a chance. But if you run with this man, your guilt becomes even more. When we catch you, which we will, all will go very hard for you."

"I'm not guilty," Dana said, lifting her chin and pushing her wet, clinging hair from her face. "And I wouldn't be able to get fair treatment in Porte Ivoire. Certainly not now."

"You are flouting the law, mademoiselle, and you will be sorry...very sorry."

Kantana was right about that. Dana was regretful already. About everything. But she was in so deep, there was no turning back, nothing to do but see it through to the end.

They heard footsteps trampling through the brush in the distance. "Keep it quiet," Alex warned Kantana. "I want to take him by surprise."

"You won't kill me, Alex," Kantana said, "even if I call out to warn him. We have been friends too long."

"Maybe I won't kill you, but I could hurt you, Jean Luc. As for your buddy, I'll kill him without a moment's hesitation. He and I are *not* friends. So I suggest you keep silent."

Dana staggered to her feet. She believed every word that Alex said. He would shoot. Kantana must have believed him, too, for he was quiet as his deputy straggled into camp, shouting that the boat had vanished around a bend in the river. Then he saw them. He stopped short, looked at his rifle but didn't raise it. Alex had him covered.

"Drop the gun and hold out your hands. The lady will handcuff you, and you'll join your boss."

Somehow it all happened as Alex said even though Kantana continued trying to convince Dana that she was making a terrible mistake going with Alex. She made a determined effort not to listen.

Once the two policemen were side by side on the ground, she and Alex were free to leave, and he was giving orders again. "Grab our gear, Dana. We'll pack the canoe and get out of here."

"And leave them—like this? They could die."

"She is correct," Kantana cut in smoothly. "And surely mademoiselle knows the penalty for killing a police officer."

"Alex—" Dana began.

"It'll never happen," he told her. "Kantana has the handcuff keys on him. Eventually they'll work themselves free and walk down the river to the next village. I'll leave them one of the guns for protection. But getting free will take time, and without a boat, they have no way to follow us. That was a brilliant move on your part." He gave her a pat on the bottom that resulted in a withering look from Dana.

"Now let's get going," he commanded.

They made two trips to the canoe, carrying supplies, all the while being watched by Kantana, his gaze no less than murderous, Dana thought.

"How'd they find us?" she asked Alex as they trekked toward the river.

"It wasn't so tough. They knew we were on the run. My guess is that Kantana heard from Mac McQuire—"

"That name's familiar."

"He gets around," Alex said flatly. "I ran into him when I was looking for Gabriel. Mac probably went into Porte Ivoire and told Kantana he'd seen me in a village on the Lomami. Kantana's no fool. He put it all together, figuring we'd travel upriver. All he had to do was follow."

"So now everyone knows where we're headed."

"Looks like it, but we can't worry about that now. Is the camp clear?"

"I think so," she answered, "but I don't want to go back to check. I hate the way Kantana looks at me, as if I'm the world's biggest criminal. If looks could kill—"

Alex laughed. "Just part of his charm. I'll check the campsite, and then we're off. If we're lucky, we might still be able to reach Mgembe territory before dark."

Dana nodded. She was already tired at barely nine in the morning. "I feel like I've lived a lifetime since sunrise."

"Since half an hour after sunrise," Alex corrected. "Remember? It took me that long to get you out of the sleeping bag." He gave her another pat, this time on the shoulder.

"Never mind when I got up. It's still only nine o'clock and I'm exhausted. I can't take many more days like this, Alex. I really can't."

He slipped his arm around her shoulder, and Dana didn't attempt to move away. She was simply too tired.

"You're doing great, Dana. You saved us."

For a moment she felt a rush of pride. "'Course, I didn't have much choice. What else could I have done?"

He gave her shoulder a squeeze. "You could have run away. Hidden. Given up. You didn't do any of those. You were remarkable."

"What I was, Alex, was scared. No, terrified," she admitted in a burst of emotion. "And in my terror, I did what I had to do. Now what I really want is for all of this to be over."

He put both arms around her and held her against him. Dana put her arms around his waist. The embrace was a haven from the horror of the past two days. She relaxed in it and felt comforted. He smoothed her damp hair away from her face the way a parent might touch a child. She rested her head against his shoulder and let out a deep, shaky breath. All the tension seemed to drain out of her.

"This will be over soon," he promised. "Nothing lasts forever." He released her. "Now, let's get a move on."

She looked at him. "There's one more thing I want."

"Name it. Food, water, a change of clothes?"

"All those, sure, but this is more important. I'd like you to quit giving orders. You're not the great powerful, all-knowing *bwana,* and I'm certainly not your devoted, adoring servant. We're in this together. I want to be treated as a partner. An equal one," she added.

Dana thought she saw a grin beginning at the corner of Alex's mouth, but if so, he controlled it quickly. "You're absolutely right," he answered seriously. "You're one hell of a good partner, and I'm proud of you. And grateful. If it hadn't been for your quick thinking, we'd both be trekking back to Porte Ivoire under police guard." He looked at her. "From now on, if I seem to be getting high-handed and authoritative, you let me know."

"Count on it," she said. "Now, if you'll check the camp for any more gear, I'll untie the boat. We've wasted enough time."

Alex didn't try to conceal his laughter. It echoed down the river. "I can see that this trip is going to get more interesting by the mile."

"YOU'RE NOT PADDLING, Dana. What's the problem?"

She dropped her paddle and turned to look at him. "My hands. I need some more of that salve."

Alex looked at the sky. Not quite noon yet. Too early to stop for a meal, but she looked beat. Maybe if they pulled up now and doctored her hands, they'd make better time in the afternoon. He steered toward the bank.

"We'll have a cup of coffee and some lunch. And I'll look at your hands."

"Sorry for the delay," Dana said as the canoe eased onto the bank. She jumped out and efficiently secured the anchor rope. Alex watched with respect. She was doing a good job.

He stepped into the shallows and waded ashore with no illusions of being dry or clean until they reached Nairobi. This was the jungle, and soon the afternoon rain showers would begin, torrential downpours that drenched to the bone. He wondered if Dana knew about those. She'd learn soon enough.

She was scouting around for twigs to start the fire when he walked over to her. "Let me see."

She held out her hands. Alex took them in his own. "The blisters look better, but where'd you get these cuts?"

There were deep gashes along her arm. "I don't know. Wait. On the propeller. I must have cut myself when I pulled off the gas line. I didn't even notice—"

"You disconnected the gas line?"

She nodded.

Alex shook his head in amazement. "More good thinking, partner. Now let's take care of your hands. Do you have any extra clothes you can tear up to wrap

around them? Like a petticoat? Doesn't the school-
marm usually rip up her undergarments to make bandages?"

"You've seen too many American Westerns. I only
have one change of clothes, and I'm not tearing up a
single thread," she said stubbornly. "It's your fault for
not letting me bring extra clothes."

He laughed at the accusation in her voice. "Okay,
okay. I'll tear up one of my shirts."

A few minutes later her hands were smeared with
ointment and wrapped with strips of Alex's T-shirt. She
sipped her coffee as he poured boiling water over pow-
dered soup.

"Meals in minutes," he joked.

"That's what I've been wondering about you," she
mused.

"That I'm such a good cook?" he teased.

"No, that your English is so idiomatic . . . and American. I thought you were French."

"I am. Born in France. But there's a catch. I had an
American mother, and you know the power American
women wield. My French father was putty in her hands.
We moved to the States when I was five. I was reared on
TV, pizza and baseball, just like any other American
kid."

"Where did you live?"

"All around," he answered vaguely. "New York
City, Boston, Denver. I saw a great deal of the country."

"But you left the States. Why?"

Alex stirred the soup and motioned for Dana to hold
out her cup. She was still full of questions, and answering them—at least partially—was probably easier than
trying to put her off.

"I wanted to see the world, travel, find my roots. Eat escargot and truffles. Watch the sunrise over Cannes. Roam the Left Bank."

She gave a rueful smile. "Choose any of the above? But why did you *really* leave?"

"My French side pulled me back. But you want the truth, right?"

Dana nodded.

"There were more opportunities for my line of work in Europe."

"Oh."

He looked up from his soup, surprised. "Just 'oh'? No penetrating questions about the specifics?"

"You wouldn't tell me the truth anyway," she answered cynically.

Alex chuckled. "You see, we can get along, Dana. All we have to do is understand each other."

"I can't imagine that will ever happen," she said emphatically.

Alex shrugged. "Maybe not, but I'd like to try."

She looked at him suspiciously. "It makes me nervous when you sound so damned sincere."

He grimaced slightly. "You're cutting close to the bone, Dana."

She smirked in self-satisfaction.

"Now I have a question for you," he said.

"We did this last night," she reminded him.

"New question, new topic," he said easily. "How come you hung around to rescue me when you could have stolen Kantana's boat and set out on your own?"

She paused, thoughtful. "I never considered stealing the boat. Where would I have gone?"

"To the Mgembe," Alex said. "You might have made it on your own, but you chose to stay and risk your life rescuing me."

Dana wrapped her arms around her knees and took her time, answering honestly.

"I did panic at first. I thought about running, but I stayed for...humanitarian purposes," she finished with a grin.

"Humanitarian?" Alex raised his eyebrows sardonically. "How warm and personal."

Dana shrugged. "Besides, I never really intended to leave you behind. Instinctively, I must have realized how much I needed you. Without you, this journey seems impossible."

"I don't know whether to feel flattered or not," Alex said, rubbing his hand across his stubbled chin. "What *did* you intend?"

"I'm not sure," she said, and they both laughed.

"In the final analysis, I guess we're stuck with each other, Dana."

"Guess so." Her blue eyes were fixed on him, unwavering, and the expression on her face was very serious. "What about you, Alex?"

"Would I have left you?" He repeated the question to give himself time to think. "No," he said. He saw her breathe a sigh and felt compelled to qualify his response. "But not because of my humanitarian feelings, either. I wouldn't have left because I need you."

He wasn't surprised when her mouth tightened. He waited for an angry reaction.

"Thanks, Alex," she said finally. "I think that's the first honest thing you've said to me."

They were both quiet, surrounded by the sounds of the rain forest. Alex knew that things had changed between them. The balance had somehow shifted. Her anger had dissipated, replaced by a tenuous connection of trust and respect. That was what he'd wanted all along—to be connected to Dana, to have her trust him. But he didn't realize that it would work both ways.

His feelings for her had begun to change, too.

THAT MOOD of camaraderie continued as they moved along the river, paddling fluidly. With her hands bound and her muscles somewhat rested, Dana got into the rhythm easily.

The monotony was relieved by a constant change in scenery along the riverbank, and soon Dana was fascinated by it, so much so that the first blurred movement in the heavy greenery caught her eye but didn't even register. Then she saw it again, flashes of light and dark as something, or someone, raced along the bank, following the boat, keeping pace with it on shore.

She pointed with her paddle, silently, and Alex responded immediately. "Got it. Keep on paddling."

A surge of excitement and adrenaline helped Dana keep up the synchronized paddling even while she watched the riverbank. There it was again! A flash of movement, and then another. She focused more intently and recognized human figures. Two tiny men with reddish brown skin, naked except for loincloths that seemed to be made of leaves or bark. Their feet were bare, but they kept up easily with the canoe as more figures joined the chase.

"Head for the bank," Alex said. "We'll make camp."

Dana's heart pounded with excitement. They'd made it, and found the Mgembe! Or maybe the Pygmies had found *them*. It didn't matter. She forgot about Kantana and his pursuit, the Porte Ivoire jail, the horrors of the last few days.

Their canoe eased against the riverbank and Dana looked around, peering into the heavy foliage. Nothing but trees and vines, twisted roots and tangled branches.

The Pygmies had vanished.

Chapter Seven

Alex secured the boat while Dana sat still, holding her paddle.

"They just disappeared into thin air," she said, almost to herself. "One moment they were here, the next moment..."

"It's not magic, Dana. They're jungle people, and they use the wilderness to suit their purposes."

"But..."

"Help me unload," he ordered, "and just act natural."

"This is wonderful, camping right among them."

"Our plan was to find the Mgembe. Well, we've found them."

"And they're watching us. I can feel their eyes following my every move."

"So far you haven't made any moves, Dana. Come on and give me a hand."

She got out of the boat and stepped onto the riverbank, trying her best to act natural. "Why don't they show themselves?"

"They will. On the other hand, maybe they won't," Alex equivocated.

"Well, that's encouraging," she said sarcastically.

Alex began to gather wood for their fire. "They could decide they don't like the way we look and just—vanish." He handed her a pot and his canteen of water. "Your turn to cook."

Dana looked through the bag of dried food, trying to concentrate and appear normal. She wanted the Pygmies to reappear, and at the same time she couldn't help being afraid. Her father had described the tribe as gentle and friendly, but not everyone agreed with that description.

"How about stew tonight?" she asked Alex, extracting a box of dried ingredients.

"Sounds good to me."

After Alex lit the fire, he began to set up their tent. Dana filled the pot, then sat back waiting for it to boil— and for the Pygmies' next move.

It was several minutes before she realized that she really *was* being watched. Alex had stopped his work and stood very still beside the unfolded tent. She forced herself not to move, keeping her head steady and looking up only with her eyes.

The Pygmy was at the edge of their campsite. She'd never seen anyone stand so motionless, like a sturdy little tree planted in the midst of the forest. He ignored Alex and stared directly at Dana with wide black eyes. She recognized what he held in his hand immediately. It was a lethal-looking blowgun, very much like the ones sold in the Porte Ivoire shops, like the one she'd been accused of using to murder Louis.

"Act natural," Alex said in a low voice.

"Sure," Dana replied, still not moving. "That's easy in the middle of the Congo, on the run from police, watched by a Pygmy who just might shoot me with a poisoned dart." But as she spoke she moved, just a lit-

tle at first, setting the pot in the center of the fire. When
that didn't seem to bother their visitor, she emptied the
contents of the package into the boiling water and
stirred. From the corner of her eye, she watched him
watching her.

"You might try saying something," Alex suggested,
keeping his voice low and conversational.

"Not all that easy, Alex. My father's notes are in my
backpack, along with the tape recorder, and any vo-
cabulary he wrote down has gone completely out of my
head."

"Think," he commanded.

"You're giving orders again," she reminded him in
a soft voice. "And not very sensible ones. If I try a word
or a phrase, it might be the wrong one. I'll just get my
pack—"

"No," he said emphatically. "That's not a good idea.
Our friend might think you're reaching for a weapon."

"You're right." Dana kept busy with the meal,
studying the little man under lowered lashes. His skin
gleamed reddish brown in the late afternoon sun. Atop
his four-foot frame, black hair curled wildly. He had
short legs, a long torso and a slight potbelly, almost like
a child. But there was nothing childish about him. He
was a man in miniature, and his blowgun was very real.

"Pull apart that loaf of Gabriel's bread and give me
a chunk," Alex said.

She did as she was told and he held the bread toward
the Pygmy, speaking first in French and then in a language that Dana couldn't understand.

"What did you say?" she whispered.

"I was trying one of the local Porte Ivoire dialects,
but I don't think he understands. Your expertise is all
we have."

"Unfortunately, my expertise is packed away. But I have an idea." She stood up very slowly, took off her necklace and held it out, her father's ivory carving dangling from the chain.

The Pygmy's eyes were suspicious, and his small body was tense and poised to move. Cautiously, she took a step toward him, the carving swaying hypnotically from her fingers.

"Dana." Alex's voice was low and angry. "What the hell—"

"Be quiet," she ordered, surprising herself at the determination in her voice. "I believe this is our best chance. When he sees what it is—" She broke off in midsentence as the Pygmy abandoned his statuary stance and moved toward her.

Slowly they approached each other. There was no doubt in Dana's mind that he recognized the ivory carving and wanted to see it more closely. When they were no more than a few feet apart, Dana looked into his eyes, which were now bright with curiosity. She tried a tentative smile but got no response. Then she took a step closer, the hand that held the necklace no more than a foot from him.

"Here. Look at it. This was given to my father by your people." She knew he couldn't understand, but she felt the need to talk to him, somehow reassure him.

In the past few days, Dana had gone through more heart-stopping experiences than in her whole life, but nothing compared to this moment, standing so close to a member of the tribe that had fascinated her father. She was excited, and suddenly she wasn't at all afraid.

The Pygmy reached out gingerly and touched the ivory carving, his fingers close to hers. She could have easily touched him. But she didn't dare. It was his move.

Then, so quickly that she didn't have a chance to react, his nimble fingers snatched the necklace from her hand, and he whirled, running toward the forest. In the blink of an eye he was gone.

Dana stood, mouth open, her empty hand outstretched. Alex was beside her in two long strides. "Great work," he said bitterly. "That piece of ivory was our passport to good relations with the Mgembe. Now it's gone."

Dana, still stunned by what had happened, snapped at him. "He'll take it to his people, and they'll recognize it, just as we'd hoped. It's just happening a little differently from the way we'd planned."

"Very differently, Dana. He's just one man. He could keep running and never show it to anyone else. This might have been our only chance."

She turned angrily on him. "What were you planning to do before you knew about the carving, Alex? You didn't even see it until I was out of jail."

"You're right," he agreed, no longer angry. "I overreacted when he ran into the jungle. But the talisman was our ace in the hole."

"And I acted too soon," she admitted.

"Maybe." He softened his voice. "But who really knows? It's impossible to second-guess the Pygmies. Sorry to take it out on you."

"You did, didn't you?" Before he could respond, she added, "And I'm also sorry that I blasted back."

"We're both on edge," he said as he took her place at the fire, stirred the stew and spooned it into two cups.

"It's so frustrating, not to know where they are and if we'll ever see them again. And if we don't, we may never get out of here to that warm bath and cool bed in the Nairobi hotel."

"We'll get there. I promised you, and I always keep my word," he said smoothly.

Dana sank down on the ground. "Liar."

He ignored the comment and handed her the cup of stew. "Here, eat this." They both began to spoon the stew into their mouths hungrily. "First we eat," he said between mouthfuls, "and then we wait. I don't know what else to do."

"The hunting party is probably miles from here," she said glumly.

"Or very close, watching us." He looked at her across the fire. "You know there's a myth that Pygmies can make themselves invisible."

"Which can probably be explained by the way they blend into the forest."

"That's the teacher in you talking."

Dana laughed agreeably. "The teacher believes the myth." She stared at the dense foliage above the riverbank. Nothing moved. The silence was eerie. "They're supposedly the oldest inhabitants in Africa. I wonder if that's true."

Alex shrugged. "It's possible. What we do know is that they have the skill to survive in the depths of the rain forest, which no other humans can do. They could have been here for longer than anyone, and we know that they're great trackers. That's why we need them. Or needed them," he amended.

Dana grimaced at the implied reproach. "I wish I'd never shown the talisman to him."

"It's okay," Alex offered.

"No, not just because of our plans. The medallion belonged to my father, and it had special meaning for me. Now I'll probably never see it again." She finished her dinner and got to her feet.

How was it possible, Dana wondered, to ache in so many places at the same time. Her hands still throbbed, her shoulders were sore, the muscles in her legs were stiff and her back hurt like hell. Doggedly, she tried to ignore all that and began sorting through her father's notes.

When Alex finished cleaning up after dinner he walked over, stood beside her and put his hand on her shoulder. "You can do that later," he said. "I know you're beat."

"*Later* I'll be fast asleep. It's now or never. I'm going to look over these notes and remember everything I read. Then I'll keep them with me from now on. I'll even sleep with them. I won't get caught unawares again." Dana peered once more into the endless green. "Maybe we'll get lucky. Maybe they'll come back."

She didn't want to contemplate the alternative. No Pygmies meant no guides out of the Congo, which meant the two of them trying to follow vague and probably inaccurate maps through forests, across rivers, into swamps.

"It could happen," Alex said. "We've been lucky so far."

She bit back disagreement. Was it luck to be attacked by hippos, almost captured by police, robbed by the Pygmies she'd hoped would help them? She would like to have blamed Alex for everything that had happened to her, but she couldn't; she'd made her own choices along the way. Soon, she would have to make another. If they couldn't find the Pygmies, should she keep on going—or turn back and face an irate and punitive Kantana?

Which was the most frightening, she wondered, the dangers that she had left behind in Porte Ivoire or the unknown dangers that lay ahead? Alex himself was very much a part of the uncertainty. She looked at him. His shirt and trousers were stained, his hair matted, his face unshaven. He was hardly the image of the virile, sophisticated man she'd first seen in Porte Ivoire. Yet he was masculine in a different kind of way. The scent of after-shave had given way to the smell of sweat; the cool demeanor was replaced by a rugged sensuality. But one thing remained the same. Of all the unknowns that awaited her, Alex was the most dangerous of all.

THERE WAS SOMETHING about waking up in a sleeping bag that was becoming exhausting for Dana, who so far had awakened more tired than when she fell asleep. Last night had been even worse because of the dreams. Or nightmares. They'd been nonstop, surreal images, all in pursuit of Dana. Louis, pursuing her from the netherworld. Jean Luc, very much alive. Her father, who kept calling out to her. Finally, Alex, running with her, and then in pursuit of her.

She sat up, ready to tell him about the dream, and only then noticed that both he and his sleeping bag were gone. Dana hadn't heard him come to bed in the night or leave in the morning, and for a moment she wondered if he'd taken off and left her.

She curled up and closed her eyes, trying not to panic. Since she'd lost the ivory talisman to the Pygmy, he could have decided that she was no longer a worthy partner and left her stranded. It was possible, she decided, rubbing her eyes. Nothing Alex did would surprise her.

Deciding to face reality and find out whether he was still in camp or not, she struggled to a sitting position and looked out through the flap.

There he was, heaping twigs onto the embers of the fire, which had glowed throughout the night. Dana heaved a sigh, picked up her notebook and recorder, which she'd kept by her side all night, and left the tent.

He looked up from the fire as she approached, excitement concealing the fatigue on his face. "They're here."

Dana stopped in her tracks and looked around the campsite. "Where?"

"I've seen three or four of them in the bush, but they haven't come into camp. I think they're waiting for you."

"Why?"

"I don't know, Dana. I just have the feeling. They're here, but they're not showing themselves to me." He poured a cup of coffee and handed it to her.

Dana took a long sip, hoping to clear her head, and narrowed her eyes against the already blazing sunlight. "I don't see anything—"

She broke off in midsentence. They were coming toward her, six small men materializing as if by magic from the shadows of deep green foliage.

Instantly awake, she switched on the tape recorder and scanned her father's notes. She'd studied them last night, committing to memory the words that possibly could be useful, relieved that they were transcribed phonetically for easy repetition. Hoping the Mgembe could understand, Dana greeted them in their own language.

They immediately began talking among themselves. Whether they understood her or were just pleased that she had spoken, Dana couldn't be sure. All she knew was that she was thrilled to be standing here, a linguist in the classroom, finally able to put her knowledge to work—among people whose language was ancient, unchanged over centuries. She hoped she was up to the challenge.

One of the Pygmies, possibly the leader of the hunting party, stepped away from the group and spoke to her. Then he held out her necklace, offering it to her almost reverently.

Dana accepted it and thanked him in his own language. He didn't seem to understand so she held the necklace up and said, "Father. The gift of my father."

The Pygmies looked blankly at each other.

"What are you telling them?" Alex asked, keeping his own voice in a low whisper.

"I thanked them and told them the carving was a gift from my father—using words I learned last night. Problem is, their language is tonal, kind of like Chinese. The way each syllable is emphasized is as important as the pronunciation."

"So maybe you're asking him if he wants a martini?"

Dana frowned at Alex, and then tried her sentence again. And again. Finally, when the Pygmy men broke into wide grins, she realized she had made herself understood. But instead of going on she found herself searching for words, entranced by the little men. Their countenances were beatific, smiles broad, teeth shining white and black eyes dancing.

"Say something else," Alex insisted. "You've just hit pay dirt."

Dana tried her usual ploy when she came face to face with people of a different language. She pointed to

herself and said her name again and again. The conso-
nant and vowel order, the simplicity of her name,
should make it easy for them to repeat. Finally, she was
rewarded by a series of Danas rippling through the air.

By reversing the process, she learned that the leader's name was Moke. He had a bad scar along his leg,
from a predator of some kind, she imagined. If only she
had the skills to talk, really communicate. She wanted
to learn all their names, ages, families—everything
about them. She berated herself for not studying the
language thoroughly before coming to the Congo. Of
course, it had been only a fantasy, her hope to meet
members of the Mgembe tribe, a dream of her father's
to fulfill.

Alex stepped beside Dana. "Show them a map. See
if they can get us across the border into Zaire."

Dana shot him a warning look. "I have to do this at
my own pace, Alex. I can't start firing questions at them
about the map. Even if I knew how to ask."

"Do your best," he muttered. "I doubt if Jean Luc
is wasting any time getting on our trail. And he might
not be the only one."

"What do you mean by that?"

"Just show them the map, Dana."

She pulled out the map and showed it to Moke. He
gestured to the others, who studied it intently, talking
rapidly among themselves."

"What are they saying?" Alex asked.

"I have no idea," Dana replied. "But I'm recording
it. Maybe I'll be able to sort it out sometime."

"Forget sometime. Or scientific research. You're not
writing a term paper." Alex took the map from her and
traced a trail on it with his finger. "We want to cross

this river and get into Zaire. Near this mission. I think there's a swamp.''

The Pygmies looked at one another, making a puzzled mournful sound. *"Ayiii?"*

Dana took the map from him. "This is getting us nowhere. They don't understand. They've never seen a map, and this certainly doesn't look like the rain forest. You'd do better to draw it in the dirt.''

"All right,'' he said to her surprise, dropping to his knees. He drew an outline of the boat and then the Lomami, a curving line on the ground. When he pointed, the Pygmies made low humming noises. He drew a tree as Dana repeated "tree'' in their language with several intonations. They seemed to understand, but whether the map meant anything to them was impossible to tell. He drew another river. Then what Dana guessed was a swamp, except even she couldn't be sure of that, and a heap of fallen stones. She repeated that word for them. They were fascinated if not enlightened.

"Ask them if they'll take us,'' he said.

She flipped through her father's notes and with words and hand gestures, asked, "We go with you?'' She pointed to herself and Alex, to the men and then to the dirt map.

There was talk among the Pygmies and what seemed like a consensus that Alex and Dana took for mutual agreement. The Mgembe looked around the camp as if sizing up the division of labor. One kicked sand onto the fire; another picked up Alex's backpack. Alex quickly took down the tent and folded it into its case, which was immediately commandeered by another Pygmy. The departure was quick and organized.

"Pygmies are nomads," Dana commented as she stuffed her notes and tape recorder into her bag. "I guess they're wizards at the get-out-of-town-fast routine."

"Suits me," Alex said. "If we have to leave some things, it doesn't matter. I'm happy to be moving toward the border."

"Alex." Dana touched his arm. "I think there's something you should know."

He looked at her, one wary eyebrow cocked. "I'm afraid to ask."

"From what I can figure out, they're taking us somewhere, but I don't have a clue where. And I have no idea whether or not they understood your map."

Alex rubbed his chin, now covered with a scruffy beard. "As long as it's not back toward Porte Ivoire, I'm game. What about you?"

Dana slipped on her backpack and stood up. "I'm with you, partner."

She wasn't surprised when he gave her bottom another pat. That was getting to be a habit, and one she didn't like. "That's really sexist, Alex. Suppose I did it to you?"

"I'd love it," he told her with a laugh.

She gave him a dirty look. "Well, don't hold your breath. Meanwhile, keep your hands to yourself, especially around the Mgembe. We have no idea what habits they might find offensive."

"And we know full well what ones you do," he said. "Damn right."

AS THEY TRUDGED ALONG, Alex behaved solicitously, walking close beside her even when she began to drop back.

"How're you doing?" he asked.

"I can hardly breathe," Dana gasped. "The Mgembe are barefoot and yet they run through the forest like—"

"Antelope?" he suggested.

"Faster. But it's not just the pace that's getting to me. The air is so humid." She lifted her blouse away from her sticky skin and fanned herself, creating the only breeze in the forest.

"Not like hiking in Colorado." He stopped to wait for her. "'Course the altitude there is a detriment. It must be difficult to keep a good pace in such thin air."

"I'll take altitude to humidity any day."

Ahead, slowing to wait for the two stragglers, the Pygmies began to sing and clap their hands.

"It's like a whole other world. No, another planet," she corrected. "I just can't believe I'm finally here among these people. I've actually talked to them, Alex, and now they're taking us—well, I'm not sure where. But we're following."

"Or you might say we're being chased."

Dana didn't want to think about that. "Just look up, Alex. These trees are incredible."

He followed her gaze upward. "The rain forest is always a surprise. Very different from the dense growth closer to the river."

Slivers of sunlight filtered through the branches of trees that soared hundreds of feet above them. The air trapped below the green canopy was heavy with moisture. She could smell the rich, fecund earth. Giant vines twisted and twined like huge green snakes around tree trunks, tendrils straining toward the sun. The carpet of the forest wasn't an impenetrable jungle of undergrowth as Dana had imagined. Instead, it was covered by leaves, and the vegetation was sparse. Moss, mushrooms and various kinds of algae hid among the curving roots.

"Look, Alex, there're palms and fig trees!" she exclaimed. "Not as monstrous as the mahoganies but big enough."

Alex nodded mutely but couldn't help smiling at her enthusiasm.

"And ferns! It's like a huge terrarium down here, but then when you look up, it's like being in a cathedral. There's something almost spiritual about it." She gazed at the great tent of leaves high overhead where occasional rays of sunlight sparkled like diamonds on the damp leaves.

"You like the Mgembe. You like the forest. And of course, you're crazy about your guide."

"Or captor, whichever fits," she retorted.

"But you admit being crazy about him?"

Dana stumbled over a huge root protruding from the mossy earth.

Alex reached out and caught her. "Falling for him?"

She pulled away. "Yes, I like the Pygmies and the rain forest, and if I was a tourist, I'm sure I'd find you an excellent guide. As it is, I'm trying to adapt. And to keep up." She quickened her pace, following the singing and clapping Mgembe.

"What's all that noise about?" Alex asked.

"It sounds to me like they're just having a great time entertaining one another, but I read that if they're not hunting, the Pygmies clap and sing to keep the wild animals away. I hope they do a damned good job," she added fervently.

"I'll go along with that, especially since I heard elephants trumpeting earlier."

"Alex—"

"In the distance," he assured her.

"They're probably as dangerous as hippos. They stampede, don't they? And trample people!"

"Don't worry. The Pygmies are great hunters."

"Hurry," she said, forging ahead. "Let's keep up with them, just to be safe."

Alex laughed as he followed after her, admittedly panting a little himself in the steamy heat.

As for Dana, he had to admit that she was doing great, probably because she was in shape. He'd never been much of an advocate of clean living, at least not the kind that included exercise and a sensible diet, but her good life-style, hiking and kayaking in Colorado, was paying off.

Her ability to take care of herself appealed to him. So did her intelligence. The women in his life had always been smart, and she was definitely one of the brightest. Otherwise, he couldn't imagine being involved....

Involved? Alex savored the word. Sure, he and Dana were involved—in their life-and-death flight across the rain forest. But the word had other connotations. There was, after all, such a thing as sexual involvement.

Alex slowed down as he thought about that. It conjured up a memory of the kiss they'd shared. He'd kissed a hell of a lot of women, yet that one kiss with Dana had been different. It had been compelling and sensual and filled with promise. For a moment, he let the memory wash over him. The taste of her. Her tongue against his. The feeling of her. Her breasts against him. The sharp edge of desire he felt was more than physical. He wanted to know her, truly know her.

Maybe he was so damned intrigued because he had no idea where he stood with her. He knew that in some way she appealed to his reckless infatuation with the unknown, that old pull toward what he couldn't possess. But there was more to Dana. More to why he wanted her.

And she was doing her damnedest to keep him at a distance. He wanted more than a view of her walking away from him, even though he couldn't deny the sight was interesting, swaying hips, slim straight back, bright golden hair. On the uneven footing of a slippery and wet path, she bounced along beautifully.

"What's the matter, can't you keep up?" she asked over her shoulder.

His smile was wicked but his answer was serious. "I like the view from back here."

With that she slowed down and walked beside him, not letting the conversation drift to the personal. "How far to the border?" she asked.

"Four, five days."

"And then we fly into Kenya?"

Alex nodded. "There's an abandoned mission across the border in Zaire. My connection will meet us there at the arranged time. If we're not there on day one, he'll come back the next day and the next..."

"Indefinitely?"

"I wish, but no. Eventually, he'll figure we were victims of the rain forest."

"But we won't be, will we?" she asked. "Not with the help of our friends, the Mgembe."

"Dana, don't be too sure that they're our friends."

"Of course, they are. You saw how they behaved with me. And listen to them now, singing and clapping—"

"You said yourself, that's to keep away wild animals."

Laughter drifted to them from the procession ahead.

"Hear that? They're happy people, and they treat their friends kindly."

"But they eat their enemies."

"Don't be ridiculous. They aren't cannibals." She stopped dead and looked at him. "Are they?"

"Let's stay friendly and we won't have to find out," Alex answered equivocally.

She started walking again as the Pygmies ran along ahead, continuing their spirited singing and clapping, and the whole jungle seemed to respond. Birds squawked and monkeys squealed. Insects buzzed. And Alex began to whistle.

Dana sighed in satisfaction. "Despite everything, I wouldn't have missed this part of the adventure. But," she added, "I'll be glad when we get to the plane. I guess the pilot expects to see Louis at the rendezvous."

Alex nodded.

"I still can't believe he's dead—or that I'm accused of his murder."

Alex groaned inwardly. Beautiful. Kissable. And persistent. Now it sounded as if she wanted to resurrect the whole Bertrand murder. That he wasn't going to do. "We need to concentrate on staying alive, Dana, not discussing the dead."

"Louis was your friend, or so you said."

"He was. But talking about his murder isn't going to bring him back."

"I know, but—"

"Conserve your breath. We've got a long way to go." He took her hand and pulled her along. "And we're about to lose our guides."

The Mgembe had crested a gentle rise and disappeared. Dana dropped Alex's hand and took off at a trot.

"Wait a minute," he said, hurrying after her.

Just when Dana thought she couldn't take one more step—but kept going rather than let him see how tired she was—she heard women's voices singing. The Pygmy camp was just ahead.

They followed the men up to a cleared oval area surrounded by huts that looked to Dana like tropical igloos shingled with green leaves. As they entered the camp, the smoke from a wood fire curled around them, and the scent of roasting meat invaded their senses. The villagers had gathered for dinner, but they moved away at the sight of the intruders—and Dana heard the word *muzungu* repeated again and again.

"It means foreigner," she told Alex, "but I think intruder would be more like it," she added as the villagers dropped back, staring silently. Many of the women and children turned and ran while the men looked away, trembling. She could hardly blame them. They'd probably seen few white people before.

And now here they were confronted by a tall, muscular but very disheveled Frenchman with a hairy face and a very blond female with slim pale legs, as sweaty as the man. The Mgembe didn't seem to be affected by the sticky heat; there wasn't a drop of perspiration on their copper-colored skin.

The silence was broken when Moke spoke to the tribe. Dana had no idea what he was saying, but her tape recorder caught it all. His words must have been comforting because the Mgembe began to return, tentatively at first, and then, as he reassured them, closer.

Finally, small hands reached out, curly heads bobbled at shoulder level, friendly faces became creased by huge smiles, and laughter rang out. Her ivory carving was examined over and over again as voices babbled excitedly around her.

Moke brought forward a small, shy woman. "Loku," he said, pointing to her.

Dana repeated the name and was rewarded by a slight smile from the woman.

"Dana," Moke went on, pointing at her.

Dana smiled with delight and shot a look of triumph at Alex. She was communicating with the Mgembe, on a primitive level.

"I think Loku is his wife," she said softly to Alex. "Pygmies are monogamous. At least that's what I've read."

Loku gingerly moved closer and studied Dana's blistered hands, now free of bandages.

"Is she going to heal you?" Alex asked.

"I think so. I caught the word *dawa,* which means medicine or herbs. Of course, it also means casting spells. I could be in trouble."

"You're doing great," he complimented. "Just stay cool."

She tried. A dozen children were now crouched in a semicircle around her, watching every move.

Loku slipped away and then reappeared with an earthen pot. She showed the smelly mixture inside to Dana. *"Dawa,"* she said, pointing to Dana's hands. Without hesitation, Dana held them out and let Loku rub in the soothing ointment.

"Do you think it'll work?" Alex asked warily.

Dana nodded. She knew instinctively that her hands would be healed.

"What next?" she mouthed at him.

Alex shrugged. "You're the attraction. Go with it."

Dana allowed herself to be led to what she presumed was a place of honor at the center of the gathering, where she sat on a pile of leaves.

"This is the meeting place where they have meals and get together for important occasions," she told Alex. "I think it's called the *baraza*."

To Dana's surprise, Moke recognized her pronunciation and smiled broadly. *"Baraza,"* he repeated, *"baraza."* Other tribesmen said the word with him.

The women gathered around Dana, piling huge quantities of food in front of her.

"Look at all this," she said to Alex.

"I'm looking. And I'm starving."

"Come and sit down. I'm sure they won't mind."

"Let's see what happens." He took his place on the leaves beside her. But he couldn't wait for a reaction and immediately began eating, spurred on by the laughter of the Mgembe, who had begun to come forward again.

While they laughed at Alex, they gathered around Dana, peering intently into her eyes.

"I'm not crazy about being stared at," she told him.

"Eat and ignore it," he advised.

Hungry enough to take his advice, she tried a few tentative bites of the roasted meat. Even though the Mgembe watched every move, Dana began to relax. After all, they had every right to be curious.

Moke named each dish as she tasted. The roasted meat was called *sondu*.

"It's one of a variety of forest antelope," Alex told her. "Which is probably my last bit of knowledge for the night."

Another kind of antelope, *sindulu*, was cooked in a stew of mushrooms and leaves. And there was a dish that reminded Dana of spinach, and a drink that they gave up trying to identify by name.

"Too many vowels in that word," Alex said. "But whatever it is, it tastes great. I guess fermented sap of some kind."

"Ugh."

"Taste it," Alex prodded. "You're adventurous."

Finally, she did. "I taste berries, nuts, herbs . . ."

"Fermented sap," he said definitely.

She laughed. "You're not going keep me from drinking it—because it's good."

"Then drink up. You might even get a little buzz before the evening's out. Then who knows what might happen?" He smiled suggestively.

"Alex, we're guests here."

"These people are pretty happy. I expect lovemaking is high on their agenda."

She gave him a poke in the rib, observed by a few of the Mgembe, who went into more gales of laughter.

"I bet that familiar wifely gesture on your part will result in something very interesting," he commented.

"I hate to ask, Alex, but what do you mean?" she said suspiciously. "I don't like the gleam in your eye."

"It's time for bed. We're both tired, and I suspect they've picked out a special hut for us."

"I suspect," she said sweetly, "there's a bachelor's hut for unmarried men."

"You wouldn't encourage that, would you, Dana, not after our being together for all this time? I can't sleep without you beside me."

"Sure you can. Anyone can get used to anything."

"You're all heart," he complained. "Uh, here come our hosts. I think the decision about who sleeps where is theirs."

THERE WERE THOSE *who came to Africa in search of a simpler way of life. The sun shone every day, food grew on trees and vines for the taking, the rivers and jungles were breathtakingly beautiful. In many ways it was an Eden.*

Yet even in paradise, money counted. No one knew that better than I. And there never seemed to be enough. Hard work was not its own reward, contrary to popular belief. Most of us only earned enough to get by, to struggle on, beyond reach of what we really wanted.

But sometimes in a wild stroke of luck, fate intervened and dangled a fortune in front of your eyes. And nothing else mattered but claiming that fortune. Not lying or stealing. Or murder.

Chapter Eight

He woke up wanting her. Which was no surprise to Alex because he'd also gone to bed wanting her. He turned over. She was curled up beside him in the hut where they'd spent the night at Moke's insistence. Dana hadn't wanted to hurt the man's feelings, and the outcome was fine with Alex. Except it was also very frustrating.

He looked away, avoiding the early morning trace of sunlight that caressed her face. It wouldn't be a good idea to get caught up in that, especially with the constant aching need inside of him. Thoughts of her were taking up too much of his mental time. The tension between them needed resolution, and for him there was only one way to achieve that. But Dana had other ideas.

Somehow he'd have to change her mind. He closed his eyes and went back to sleep.

A scratching noise woke him, and Alex was immediately on guard. But it was only Dana pulling at the branches that formed the hut.

"What the hell are you doing, trying to destroy the place?" he asked, crawling out of the tiny hut.

"I'm trying to figure out how they do this. It seems simple enough. They bend the saplings into a dome and make a lattice framework. The whole thing is covered with leaves. Mongongo leaves," she spoke into her tape recorder. "But it's more intricate than it looks. They're layered like tiles."

"Mongongo leaves? You're really into this," he observed.

"I might as well learn all I can while we're here."

Alex shrugged. "Learn fast. We aren't going to be around that long. Did you talk to Moke last night about leading us across the border?"

"Nope."

"Dana," he warned, "we need to get out of here—"

"I'll ask," she promised. "Go have breakfast while I finish up here."

"Aren't you going to eat?"

"I already did."

"I must have been more tired than I thought if you were up and about before me."

"The macho man overslept," she teased.

He let that one go, not about to tell her of his early morning frustrations. "The macho man is stiff and sore from sleeping on the ground, and he, too, is looking forward to a hotel bed. What's for breakfast?"

"Honey." Her voice was guileless, but he saw the devilish grin.

"And?"

"That's it. Honey. Oh, and parts of the hive, the dead bees, some larvae. You'll love it."

"Can't wait," he teased back. "It sounds worthy of a four-star Parisian restaurant."

She returned to studying the leaves and the pattern they formed. Alex stood for a long time in the open doorway of the hut, looking at her. She'd given up on doing anything with her hair and pulled it back in a careless ponytail. Tendrils escaped haphazardly and curled around her face. There were dirt and grass stains on her clothes and scratches from briars and fallen limbs on her legs. She seemed oblivious to them all.

He was thinking again about how much he wanted her when she turned and saw him staring. "I thought you were going to eat," she said.

"I am. But I wanted to ask—how are your...hands?" That was the first thing that came, not very convincingly, into his head.

"Amazingly better. Loku put some more ointment on this morning. If we had more time, imagine what we could learn about natural medicine, Alex."

"But we don't have more time," he said gruffly. As he went out, he turned and called over his shoulder, "Talk to Moke this morning, Dana. And I mean it."

DANA PLUNGED into the water with the women and children from the tribe. She could hear the voices of the men bathing around a bend in the river and chuckled to think of Alex cavorting with his miniature friends.

As the women laughed and talked and the children squealed with delight, Dana pulled off her shorts and shirt, scrubbed them vigorously and wrung them out. Still wearing her bra and panties and without feeling any inhibitions around the naked bathers, she moved closer to the bank. There she hung her clothes out to dry on the overhanging branches.

That's when she noticed that the women were watching her, giggling as she stood waist deep in the water. They began to gather around, talking rapidly to one another. She had no idea what they were saying, but it seemed to involve her lingerie, especially her bra. Then it came to her. They never covered their breasts. Joyfully, she joined in their laughter.

Without a moment's hesitation, she unhooked the bra and handed it to Loku, who examined it minutely.

"*Aas!*" Loku said as she passed it around the circle. The women studied it, put it on like a bonnet, tied it around their necks, not ever getting it quite right.

Dana let them have their fun. Still laughing with them, she dived underwater, swam to the center of the stream and surfaced, feeling clean and refreshed. When she looked back, someone had hung her bra on the branch beside her clothes.

The Pygmies' humor was full of life. She was envious of that uninhibited happiness and jealous of their unselfconscious freedom.

After a long swim she waded to shallower water and scooped up a handful of sand, which she used to scrub her skin. Then she ducked again, washing it away. The water flowed across her shoulders and breasts, down along her hips and thighs. It was wonderfully warm and sensuous and made her think of a man's hands caressing her body.

"Dammit," she said aloud. It made her think of Alex! If she closed her eyes and moved her hands up her body, she could imagine that he was touching her.

She let her body relax and flow with the water, drifting, caressing herself. Eyes closed, she floated along, downstream, until she realized that she was drifting into a fantasy and stood up quickly, shaking the water from her hair and body, ridding herself of Alex's image.

Dana struggled into her clothes, which in the jungle humidity weren't that much damper than usual. Then she followed the women, who'd formed into an irregular line and begun the trek back to camp.

As if it was planned, they converged on the men around the first turn. Alex had apparently washed his clothes, too, and put them on wet; he was bare-chested, carrying his shirt. His hair was clean and shining and his chest glistened. With his fledgling beard and mustache, he looked even more handsome—and more mysterious.

He strolled toward them, took Dana's hand and pulled her off the path, letting the others go on ahead. As soon as they disappeared around the first bend, he asked, "Have you talked to Moke?"

"Alex, I've been bathing with the women. *You* were with the men."

"Unfortunately, I can't seem to make myself understood. You can. Now, what about our plans for getting to the border?"

"I told you. I was bathing—"

"Earlier. Before you left the camp. Did you ask?"

"Not exactly."

"In other words, no?"

She stopped and faced him. "You don't understand. We're guests. I can't order them to lead us to the mission. If you knew more about the way the tribe works—"

"I don't want a lecture on Pygmy customs, Dana."

"Maybe you need one," she retorted. "They don't have tribal chiefs. They do everything with a kind of committee mentality, and they don't take kindly to strangers coming in and giving orders. Of course, I'll ask, but when the time is right." She started down the path, but he grabbed her upper arm and held her.

"We may not have time, Dana. Right this minute someone is probably following us, and if we hang around while you collect Pygmy lore and bond with Loku, we'll be in trouble."

She pulled away from him. "Kantana can't be on our trail yet. He had to get back to Porte Ivoire, organize a posse or whatever you call it—"

"He's not the only one who could be after us," Alex said flatly. "Have you thought about that?"

Alex had mentioned that possibility before and then left it dangling. He seemed to have the same agenda now—frighten her but don't explain.

"Oh, you mean the international spies who're after your secret documents?" She still couldn't buy into that story.

"Just trust me, Dana, when I tell you that we need to get the hell out of here."

"No one can find us," she countered. "The Pygmies wouldn't leave a trail."

"For God's sake stop arguing with me when you don't know what the hell you're talking about," he snarled. "You and I aren't Pygmies, are we? We've probably left a trail a child could follow."

As Dana studied his face, she realized there was real concern in his eyes. He was worried about being followed, and he was concerned about something else. Something he wasn't telling her.

With that thought, she turned and started to walk toward the camp, aware that Alex was the master of his own secrets. It was only then that she noticed how quiet everything was. The Mgembe had vanished into the rain forest, the animals were silent. Even the breeze was still. The hairs on the back of her neck began to prickle. She reached out a hand for Alex.

His voice was low and calm. "In front of you, just to the left of the path. A leopard. A big one."

Dana stifled a moan as she slowly turned her head and saw him, crouched by the path. Her first instinct was to run, to get the hell out of there. She felt herself tense, felt her muscles gather momentum as she prepared to escape the danger.

But she was blocked by Alex. His broad chest loomed in her way, and his grip was like iron on her arm. "Don't move," he said, "not even a hair." His voice was low and husky but the words were very clear.

The long, lean animal's smooth muscles were tightened into a deadly crouch. He was poised to spring! Dana tried to swallow, but her throat was dry and tight. She tried to whisper her fear to Alex, but the words wouldn't come. All she could do was stare at the magnificent beast coiled before them. He was savage and beautiful, one with the jungle—its most dangerous predator.

As Dana stood frozen, she felt the perspiration break out on her forehead and trickle down her face. She was overcome by a fear more intense than anything she'd ever felt.

Then she saw the blood. "Oh, my God, Alex," she whispered, her voice raspy. "Look at his mouth, his talons—"

Alex squeezed her hand tightly. "The blood's a good sign. He probably just made a kill and stashed the carcass. We may be in luck."

But what if the carcass was nearby and he was protecting it? Then they wouldn't be in luck, they'd be dead. Dana began to tremble all over. Her teeth rattled. She was afraid of losing control. Alex held her steady and didn't let her collapse.

They stood, arms around each other, for what seemed like hours to Dana. Then the great cat raised his head, twitched his nose and with a flick of his long tail was gone, slinking into the shadows of the rain forest.

Dana gave a sob, hid her face against Alex's chest and held on for dear life. Her fingers dug into the bare skin of his back. She was still trembling wildly. Finally, she found her voice.

"I was so scared," she cried. "So scared." She looked at him, frowning, confused. "And yet at the same time it was..." Her voice broke.

"I know," he said, holding her close.

"Do you? Do you understand?" she asked, not sure she understood herself.

"Yes." He wrapped her in his arms. Her clothes were soaking wet, and he thought he could feel every bone in her body shiver.

"That mixture of danger and excitement," she whispered, "was like nothing I've ever felt."

"I know exactly what you mean." He caught his hands in her wet hair and lowered his lips toward hers. "The danger that makes your heart pound, the excitement that heats your blood. It's called being alive, Dana."

She pressed herself more tightly against him. He felt her nails dig into his flesh almost violently. He brought his mouth down on hers with a terrible kind of force.

Dana reacted with such feeling that Alex's head reeled. Her need was palpable. He felt it on the surface of her skin, tasted it on her lips as she opened to him.

He wanted her desperately, wanted to own her, to possess every inch of her body. He wanted to make love to her—here on the path. To hell with the danger. He craved the excitement of taking her—now.

Dana knew what was happening but was helpless to stop it. He was dark, handsome and very dangerous, possibly even deadly, and she was on fire for him. She couldn't control the feelings any more than she could control her hands, her lips, her tongue in their response to him. Or what was happening to her nipples, taut against him. Or the throbbing warmth between her legs that ached for him.

She couldn't control any of that and didn't even try. In fact, she insinuated one of her legs between his so that she could be closer. Her head whirled. She was hot and dizzy with desire as he moved his hands along her body. His rough beard bruised her skin. His greedy lips claimed hers again and again.

Then suddenly he stopped kissing her, took her face in his hands and spoke in that low seductive voice that frightened at the same time it fascinated her.

"I want you, Dana. You can't pretend anymore that nothing is happening between us."

She let her cheek rest against his chest. "It's all so confusing," she cried almost desperately.

He lifted her chin and looked into her eyes. "No, you're wrong, Dana," he said gently. "It's all so simple. If you'd just let it be."

But it wasn't simple, she thought. The complicated factors included Louis, the murder, the so-called secret documents, the lies. Yet she wanted Alex with an unbounded physical intensity she'd never felt before. She pressed her lips against his bare chest. He tasted of perspiration, salt. He smelled of excitement and fear. The mixture was a powerful aphrodisiac.

It was a combination she had to get away from. She took a step back, hoping it would help. But it didn't. The trembling began again, more overwhelming than when she'd faced the big cat. She had to escape it.

In a clear voice she said, "I'll talk to Moke."

"Don't change the subject, Dana," he responded. He still held on to her arm.

"I'm not," she rebuked. "You told me we needed to keep moving. You're right." She started down the path.

Alex put his arm around her and walked by her side. "We can run for the border, Dana. But we can't escape each other. You know that now, don't you?"

Her answer was lost in the call of Moke. *"Aas aas ibude, aas aas mota,"* he cried out as he ran toward them through the trees.

"What is it, what's the matter?" Alex asked.

"Nothing's the matter. Elephants have been sighted. They're going on the hunt!"

BY LATE AFTERNOON of that same day, Dana and Alex had traveled as far as they could with the tribe. They were on their own, alone in the jungle, and the Mgembe had raced ahead after the elephant.

Dana felt a tremendous emptiness as the voices of the tribe faded into the distance.

"I'll never see them again," she said sadly, "and we owe them so much, Alex." Instinctively, she took his hand. "Moke and his tribe found us, sheltered us . . ."

"And they guided us this far, Dana."

"I know. They've made it possible for us to get close to the border. But now they're gone, and I feel as though I've lost a group of friends."

"Maybe you'll see them someday—"

"No," she interrupted Alex's thought. "Even if I ever come back to the rain forest, the chances of finding Moke's small tribe are minuscule."

"They had to go on without us, Dana," he reminded her.

"I know."

"As fond as they were of you, the elephant means everything to them. The hunt is what it's all about. For us, it's the border."

She looked at him thoughtfully. "Do you think you could have kept up with the hunters on your own, without me and all my stuff?"

Alex shook his head. "In true Americanese, no way. Besides, the Pygmies never would have led us all the way into the swamp. You said yourself that they believe a monster lives in there."

Dana laughed. "Yes, huge with a long neck and tiny head. I hope we don't run into it—if *we* ever get there."

"They got us this far. And with their directions and my map, we'll get the rest of the way. But for now, we're stopping to make camp," he announced. "I want to approach the swamp in the morning when we're fresh."

"It's okay, Alex, I can go on. I'm not tired," she lied. It seemed too soon to stop, to be alone with Alex. She could still feel the morning's kiss on her lips, still remember what it was like to be in his arms.

"We have to rest sometime, Dana." He dropped his pack to the ground and reached for hers, and when he did, his hand rested lightly on her arm. "Now is as good a time as any."

His eyes caught hers, held them. Her heart began to beat faster simply from the touch of his fingers against her arm. She was afraid of what was happening between them, but she felt powerless to stop it. All she could think of was to keep moving. "No, we have to—"

"Dana, we have to stop."

She realized that was true. They couldn't keep going forever; she couldn't keep avoiding him forever, either. "I . . . I guess so," she said.

"I'll put up the tent, unless you're planning to build a hut out of those mambo leaves."

"Mongongo," she said automatically. For a moment she wished she had the know-how to put up one of the huts. At least it would give her a place of her own to sleep—away from Alex. In fact, that wasn't a possibility. They'd be sleeping together in the tent again tonight. She couldn't run or hide from him—or her feelings.

"I'll fix dinner," she said absently, well aware, as was Alex, that there wasn't that much preparing to do. They'd brought along gifts from the Mgembe of honey, nuts, berries and fruit. All she had to do was set it out. And she took her time.

Even though she'd turned her back on Alex, she was very aware of his presence as she listened to him unpacking, moving around, setting up the tent. She thought about lying in it beside him and couldn't put the image out of her mind.

Abruptly, she got up and moved to the edge of the campsite, trying to get away from the sight and sound of him. But she could still picture him moving around, spreading the tent as he continued the ordinary job of making camp. Except there was nothing normal about it. Everything seemed magnified bigger than life. The trees soared hundreds of feet above her, their leaves greener than green. The setting sun was a ball of fire trailing across a lavender sky. The intensity was overpowering. But it wasn't frightening. Not nearly as scary as the nearness of Alex.

Once again she experienced the heady mix of fear and excitement fighting for control, shimmering on the hot air. She'd never felt more alive.

She sensed Alex standing behind her, heard his breathing, slow and regular. Did she imagine the beating of his heart, or was it hers that pounded so loudly?

She didn't have to turn around; she knew he was there. Then she looked at him over her shoulder, and he touched her hair lightly and ran his fingers along her neck. Her skin felt hot and tight, as if she was wrapped in a blanket of sensuality. She turned into his arms. His mouth found hers, and she flowed into the kiss.

There was no thought of breaking away, not even the slightest hesitation. She was where she wanted to be; this was what she'd been waiting for all day. This was what she'd wanted since the first time she'd seen him. His beard scratched her face, rough against her sensitive skin. But where the roughness ended, she felt the soft moistness of his lips. The sensation of the scratchy beard and the smooth mouth, eagerly pressing against hers, made Dana's head swim. Then his hot tongue sought and found hers.

The kiss went on and on until she felt her legs grow weak. He held her up, and with his lips against her ear, breath warm and teasing, whispered, *"Voulez-vous couchez avec moi ce soir, ma chérie?"*

"Yes, yes. Oh, yes." She felt like laughing and crying as all her emotions tumbled together.

Alex took her hand and led her to the tent. It was still spread out on the ground, unstaked. Together they knelt on it, locked immediately in another kiss. And as they kissed, their hands sought each other, frantically pulling at buttons and zippers.

Alex got her blouse off first, pulled down the straps of her bra and cupped her breasts with his strong, lean fingers. It was just as she'd fantasized. She guided his head to her breast and felt his lips on her taut, tingling nipple. A spiraling curl of passion swept through her, and she finished what she'd begun, tugging at the zipper of his pants until she touched his manhood. It was hot and throbbing against her hand. She held on, moving her fingers along its shaft.

His words came in short, harsh gasps. "Do you want to drive me wild, woman?"

"Yes," she cried as he pulled off his pants and kicked them away. "Yes, I want you to feel as wild and crazy as I do."

"Just watch me," he said, drawing her on top of him and kissing her mouth, her face, her neck. He kissed one breast and then the other. At the same time he pulled at her shorts and panties and rolled over until he was on top. Then he worked his way down her body, licking, tasting.

Dana held her breath, waiting....

She felt him slide his tongue along her skin, nibble with his teeth on her hipbone and then lick hungrily in the warm curve inside her thigh. After a few seconds, his mouth, his tongue and even his teeth found the moistness between her legs. The pleasure he created was exquisite torture. Tremors of excitement danced through her and left her breathless. Out of control, she writhed beneath him, lifting her hips toward him.

Before she could catch her breath, gasp for air, he took her again in his arms and held her close, covered her with the length of his long, hard body. He kissed her throat, her chin, slipped his tongue inside her ear.

She dug her fingernails into the smooth muscles of his back, licked his neck, tasted his salty warmth, wanting to be closer to him, curl herself up beside him, inside him. She kissed his shoulder, nibbled and then bit down on him. Being close suddenly wasn't enough. She wanted to mark him with her teeth and nails. To mark him and make him hers.

He felt pain from her branding and loved it. "You're wonderful, Dana," he said. His voice was low, hoarse, seductive against her ear. "I knew you would be." He held her closer, crushing her against him. "I want you so much. I want to be inside of you."

"Yes," she said, "yes." She caressed his hardness. "I want you, too." Her voice sounded far away, floating on the waves of passion. She shifted in his arms and guided him inside.

He filled her, inch by inch, moving slowly at first, letting the pressure build until she felt she would explode. He looked down at her, his green eyes heavy-lidded, secretive, knowing. Then he began to move, matching his rhythm to her response, thrusting more deeply until she belonged to him totally, just as he belonged to her.

Dana lost herself in the aching, blossoming need. Nothing existed except their oneness and the intensity of the exquisite pleasure. His hands slid beneath her hips and lifted her, and she felt him at her very core. She arched toward him, opened herself to him, swept along toward the sweet joy of their union.

Ripples of pleasure cascaded over her, muscles tightened, released in shuddering climax. She trembled in his arms, called out as she clung to him. And as she rode the waves of her ecstasy, she felt his tumultuous response to her, hot and wild, like the very land that had brought them together.

Dana smiled, a soft secret smile, and murmured the words she hadn't dared to speak that night in the Stanley Hotel garden. "I came to find you, my love."

BODIES DAMP with passion, limbs languid with love-making, they lay snuggled together, wrapped in the tent that was still spread on the ground. He'd wanted to put it up so they could crawl inside, but she hadn't been able to let go of him long enough. She needed to stay close, locked in his arms, touching him, feeling his warm, pliant skin against hers.

They kissed again, softly and sweetly. "Any regrets, Dana?" His breath tickled her ear.

"*Je ne regrette rien.* Isn't that what the French song says? Anyhow it's true of me tonight. No regrets at all."

"Not even the lack of a tent?" he teased.

"Nope."

"Pretty soon the insects will be nibbling at you."

"They already are," she admitted. "I'll let you put it up. But not yet. I want to hold on a little longer."

He ran his fingers down her arm, and she shivered. "Cold?"

"With your arms around me? Never. I'm shivering with passion and desire and need. All those emotions I've read about but never felt. I'm afraid you've spoiled me for any other man."

"Have I really done that?" he asked, cupping her breast and rubbing his thumb against her nipple. It hardened against his touch.

"Absolutely. You're doing it now." She closed her eyes, her face relaxed, softened, her smile content and sensual.

If she were a cat, she'd be purring, he thought. That contentment pleased him, just as her responsiveness excited him, her passion surprised and delighted him.

"Then let me spoil you for a few more nights."

"And after that," she said sadly, "I'll go home. And you'll... who knows what you'll do—or where you'll go."

"Wherever my fancy leads me. It's a big world out there. You should give it a whirl."

"That's what I'm doing!" she said. "I never meant to be in the depths of the rain forest—or in Porte Ivoire, for that matter. This is all so new to me."

"And yet you said just now that you came to find me, Dana."

"You heard? Do you think that's crazy?"

"No. I think it's wonderful."

"And true, somehow. My whole life is changing, and I keep wondering how—and why."

He kissed her lips. "That's your problem."

"What?"

"All that wondering." He kissed her again, enraptured by the taste of her, the feel of her body molded against his. "All that professorial analyzing. It's not good for you."

"And you know what's good for me, I suppose?" she asked teasingly.

"Of course I do. I know what's good for both of us." He covered her body with his. "We'll put up the tent later."

SOMETIME during the night he kept his word, waking long enough to get the tent up and staked before returning to her arms. They slept and woke again, making love gently and languidly.

Just after sunrise, he slipped away, mumbling something in her ear about reconnoitering a trail. She nodded and snuggled up in the sleeping bag, expecting to go back to sleep. But it wasn't the same without him.

Dana stretched sensuously, touched her lips, which were bruised and swollen, then moved around in the sleeping bag, trying to get comfortable. Her lips weren't the only place she was sore, she admitted to herself with a blush. She ran her hands along her body, holding onto the memories of the night as long as she could. She wouldn't let the old suspicions ruin what had happened between her and Alex. It had been special and wonderful; because of it, everything was different now.

Taking her time, Dana used a little extra water from their supply to clean up and brush her teeth. As she dressed, she found herself singing. How long had it been since she'd sung in the morning? She smiled. As a teenager, she'd sung in the shower, and from the looks of the sky, she might find herself doing just that again.

Storm clouds scudded across the sun, and the air was heavy with the scent of rain. They'd yet to face the Congo's torrential rains, but it looked like they weren't going to escape them much longer. A few drops were already coming down.

Dana ducked into the tent. She hadn't brought along any rainwear, but she imagined Alex had, since he was familiar with the jungle weather. She pulled out his backpack and unzipped it, rummaging through the clothes. Plastic rain covers were usually folded into small bundles and stuffed into a pouch. She felt into the corners—nothing but clothes, even some of hers that he'd agreed to fit into his pack.

But there was an outside compartment. She unzipped it and to her relief found a large leather bag. Good, she thought, he'd brought more than one. But when she opened the clasps, Dana found, not plastic raincoats, but layers of protective wrapping. Curious, she pulled away the cotton batting. It covered a heavy object, wrapped in a layer of tissue.

Dana held it in her hands, a frown crossing her forehead. For a long moment she knelt beside his pack, holding whatever it was, weighing it in her hands before pulling away the tissue. When she did, her fingers moved slowly, carefully, as if she was dissecting the object, layer by layer.

Then her heart jumped to her throat as she looked at her discovery, an elephant statue, about eight inches high and weighing three or four pounds, made of a shiny metal. Could it be gold? And the jewels encrusted on it, could they be diamonds, rubies and sapphires? If so, she was holding a king's ransom in her hands.

At that thought, a cold hand seemed to close around her heart. Of course, it was real. Alex wouldn't have broken her out of jail to help him sneak a worthless fake out of the country. If he'd come by the statue honestly, he wouldn't have created an elaborate subterfuge about secret agents and government terrorists to enlist her aid. It was horribly clear. He was smuggling a priceless golden statue out of the country—not secret documents!

As she stood up, prepared to scream out her anguish and betrayal to the hovering sky, Alex opened the flap of the tent. She thrust the elephant toward him. "You bastard," she shouted, "you lying bastard."

Chapter Nine

"What the hell's going on?" Alex's voice was filled with anger.

But Dana's fury matched his as she stood before him. "There were never any secret documents!"

"Wait a minute!" He reached for her arm.

"You weren't on a patriotic mission for the French government," she went on, pulling away from him. "You're a thief, Alex Jourdan. A thief!" She shook the elephant in his face.

"And what do you call yourself, Dana? What do you call a person who searches someone else's belongings?"

"I wasn't *searching*," she defended. "I was looking for a poncho. It's raining, or hadn't you noticed?"

"They're in the other compartment," he said, seemingly unperturbed. "As for the elephant, I can explain."

"I'll bet you can. Wait, let me guess. You won this in a poker game, just like the hotel." Her voice dripped with sarcasm. "Admit it, Alex," she continued, looking at the jewel-laden statue. "This is stolen property."

"You're wrong." He moved all the way into the tent, closing the flap against the rain, which had intensified.

"The Elephant d'Or belongs to the man who holds it in his hand at the moment." He took it from her. "I'm that man."

"How clever." She was amazed by his brazen response. Instead of showing embarrassment—or even anger—at her discovery, he managed to find a convenient excuse for himself. "And how did you happen to become that man?"

He smiled. "It didn't happen. It was planned. Louis—"

"Louis?" In spite of the torpid heat, made worse by the rain, Dana felt a cold shiver along her spine.

"Yes, Louis brought the elephant upriver from Brazzaville, and I—"

"And you killed him for it!" All of Dana's suspicions, pushed out of her mind when Alex made love to her, came rushing back.

"No, Dana."

"Yes, you killed Louis and took the elephant. You killed him!"

The suspicions surged into one awful moment, and she reacted instinctively, pushing past him and out of the tent, running blindly, wildly, with no thought of where she was going. All she wanted was to get away—from him. Alex had killed for the elephant and then lied to her, used her, betrayed her. Would she be the next to die?

The rain forest gave way to swampy lowlands, and as she ran Dana felt briers and vines pull at her, grab her, wrap her in their snarled tendrils. Frantically, she sped on, heart pounding, lungs screaming for air. The rain pounded against her, washing the spurts of blood from her scratched arms and legs.

Alex came out of nowhere, a powerful force that hit her from behind and brought her to the ground. At first she was stunned, the breath knocked out of her, but as soon as she regained her senses, Dana struggled frantically.

It was hopeless; his body covered hers, and he held her in a powerful grip. She could taste the mud that covered her face.

"Listen to me, Dana. You can't run away. There's nowhere for you to go."

That made her wilder, and she fought against him. "Away from you—that's where I'll go!" she cried.

"All right. If that's what you want, I'll let you leave. But first you're going to listen to me."

"What choice do I have?" she said, almost choking in the mud.

"As a matter of fact, none." He got up and pulled her to her feet. The pelting rain stung her face, washing away the mud. He dragged her under a huge tree. "Sit down," he said, "and listen to me."

She fell back against the tree trunk and dropped to the ground. Its enormous branches gave at least some protection from the rain. He sank down beside her.

"I did not kill Louis," he said emphatically. "He was my closest friend."

"Louis also had the elephant."

"That was our plan."

"And your supposed feud, that was also planned?" she asked skeptically.

"Of course. We didn't want any connection between us. When Louis removed the elephant—"

"*Removed?* Is that the new word for stole?" she asked.

"I'll never be able to explain if you keep interrupting."

Dana's response was a derisive grunt. She might as well be quiet and let him talk. "Could we at least get out of this infernal rain?"

"I wasn't sure you wanted to go back to the tent," he said.

"If I'm going to be subjected to another one of your lies, I'm damned if I'm going to do it sitting here in the rain."

He pulled her to her feet and all but dragged her back to camp. She half ran along beside him, cursing aloud. When they got to the tent, she wrenched herself from his grip and went inside.

He tossed her a towel from his recently ransacked belongings. "Louis Bertrand was a man of many talents. He got to the elephant logically, by supplying the wine for a party in Brazzaville. Of course, he brought a special bottle of brandy as a gift for the host, a wealthy and particularly specious collector. The brandy contained an additive—"

"Naturally, the evil owner of the elephant deserved to die," she said in her nastiest tone.

"At first you accuse me of killing Louis, and now you call *him* a thief and murderer."

"A type that doesn't appeal to me, dead or alive."

"For God's sake, shut up and listen. Louis only drugged the man. Then he *removed* the elephant from a cabinet where it was always stored, away from view. The next day, he took the *Congo Queen* to Porte Ivoire, hiding the prize in Father Theroux's bag."

"He used an innocent priest to carry stolen goods?"

"The priest never knew, Dana."

"That doesn't make it right," she argued. "It's never right to use another person. The way you used me," she added bitterly, "the way you used Louis to deliver the elephant. Then you killed him."

"I didn't kill him!" Alex's voice was raised to a shout; the veins in his neck protruded. His anger frightened Dana into silence. All she could do was watch him—and remember. She remembered being in his arms, making love to him, her body filled with passion. The thought of the intimacy they'd shared repelled her.

When Alex spoke again, it was in a calmer voice.

"Louis was my partner in this. When he reached Porte Ivoire, he transferred the elephant to me as planned, and since he and I were supposedly enemies, no one suspected that I had it. The killer thought it was on Louis or in his room. He—or she—found out differently. The search turned up nothing."

Dana listened without comment.

"But the killer assumed the elephant was still somewhere in Porte Ivoire, and eventually he—or she—would find it. With Louis dead and the *Congo Queen* broken down, there'd be time for a thorough search. No one counted on my involvement. Or on your knowing about the Mgembe. *Or* on us taking off together with the elephant."

After a long silence she asked, "Let me see it."

Alex reached in his pack, pulled out the statue and handed it to her. For the first time, she examined the elephant closely. Never in her life had she seen anything so exquisite. The tiny tusks were made of ivory tipped with diamonds, the eyes of sapphires that were almost purple. She turned it in her hand. The collar was studded with rubies, and a huge emerald was embedded in the golden saddle. "It must be worth—"

"It's priceless, Dana. The Elephant d'Or was made by the Portuguese in the sixteenth century, either in Africa or India. It has belonged to rajas and dukes, princes, thieves, men both good and evil. Over the centuries, it has been stolen and restolen countless times, and has no real owner. No provenance. Sales slips don't come with the elephant."

She returned it to him. "It belongs in a museum, not in the hands of criminals."

He looked at her sharply and then shrugged. "Let's just say that Louis set it free."

"And paid for that with his life," Dana replied sadly. "And you're trying to tell me that one of the people who traveled with me on the *Congo Queen* murdered him? It doesn't make sense. They're tourists, not killers, they—"

"Were all at the party in Brazzaville," he finished for her. "One of them could have known about the elephant and followed Louis to Porte Ivoire."

"Who, Millicent, for God's sake? Father Theroux? It's not possible."

"Anything is possible when such a prize is involved. Millie has lived in the Congo for years. She knew about the legend of the elephant. Hell, everyone did. As for Betty and her boyfriend, I'm sure you'll agree that together they're capable of anything."

"But they didn't know where the elephant was," she reminded him.

"Come on, Dana. An amateur could have solved that mystery. As for the murder, any of them could have learned to use a blowgun. And God knows, all of them could have used the money. But Longongo, with his contacts through the government, is my number-one suspect."

And you are mine, Dana thought. It would have been so easy for Alex, after getting what he wanted, to kill Louis and make it look as if she did it. She stopped in midthought. Not only could Alex be a murderer, he probably framed her, broke her out of jail, used her. And then what? She didn't want to think of his next move.

"You'll never be able to sell it," she said flatly. "Who would buy what you said yourself is a prize, a legend that people know about, probably all over the world."

"Remember, it's been bought and sold many times in the past. There're plenty of collectors out there who'd give a right arm for the Elephant d'Or."

"I'd think the Egyptian would want it back. Hasn't he called the police?"

"The police?" Alex repeated sarcastically. "The guy lives on the edge of the law. He's hardly the type who'd invite the police into his private dealings. Besides," he added cynically, "the police would be just as likely to rip off the elephant as anyone."

"No one should rip it off. It belongs in a museum," she insisted again. "If you had any sense of right or wrong, any honor—"

"Honor?" he scoffed. "Honor versus half a million dollars? Think again, Dana. I have as much right to this statue as anyone. It's mine now, and I'm going to hold onto it."

"I'll never understand that kind of thinking."

"I'm not asking you to," he said. "I'm just telling you the facts. Now, we'd better get going. We have a timetable to meet."

"*You* have a timetable, Alex. I don't."

"What do you plan to do, Dana, stay here in the jungle? Try to make your way back to Porte Ivoire and jail? Whether you like it or not, your best choice is with me." He hesitated a beat. "Besides, I'm taking the tent."

His humor didn't amuse her, not when she had been lied to and used. Not when the possibility was still very strong that she was traveling with a killer.

BY THE TIME they'd packed and were ready to leave camp, Dana realized that Alex hadn't put the statue back in the same place. It was hidden somewhere else, and she didn't ask where; she didn't want to know.

The rain, which had subsided for a while began again, turning their path into a stream of rushing water. It gushed around her ankles and filled her shoes, but Dana kept going, damned if she'd fall behind, even when they came to a gully that under normal circumstances would be a challenge. In the rain it was hell. But she made it across. On the far bank, she dug into the muddy foot-holes left by Alex and persevered, moving ahead—and then slipping. Just as she neared the top she slipped again—and went down, all the way down. She landed at the bottom on her backside, but when he came back to get her, offering a hand, she refused.

After a few horrendous attempts, she finally made it out, and Dana wasn't surprised that he didn't bother to acknowledge the feat. He simply moved on. Doggedly, she followed, hating him, cursing the pelting rain and herself for listening to Alex in the first place. How could she have been taken in by his secret-documents-for-the-greater-good story?

Because she'd been desperate—and in jail. Because he offered a real solution and, finally, because she *wanted* to believe him.

The rain ended suddenly, and the sun blazed from a cloudless blue sky, leaving the swamp a steamy, sweltering greenhouse. Mosquitoes swarmed incessantly in air so heavy with moisture that breathing was a challenge. Dana's clothes were wet and cloying against her skin, but she was determined not to complain to Alex. She would keep on walking until she dropped.

He followed a primitive path, pushing through undergrowth, and she tried to keep up. If she lagged behind, the wet branches that he passed would snap back and slap her in the face.

As she hurried along, Dana ducked under a particularly low-hanging tree and felt something land on her. She assumed it was a branch. But it was too heavy. It weighed her down, and when she fought for balance, she realized what had happened and let a scream from the deepest primal depths of fear and loathing.

"A snake! Oh, my God, Alex, get it off. Get it off!"

The reptile had fallen from the limb and looped itself over her shoulders. She could feel the undulating muscles beneath its smooth skin as it slithered across her shoulders and wrapped around her neck. Fighting to free herself from the reptile, she lost her balance and fell to her knees, looking directly into the wedge-shaped head and flickering tongue. She closed her eyes and screamed again.

Alex was already beside her, and with one hand he grasped the snake behind its head. With the other he lifted it off of her, heaving it into the bushes.

Dana collapsed against him, and for one heady moment his arms were around her. "It's gone," he said. "You're all right."

Her knees were weak and shaky, and Dana prayed she wouldn't faint. "It was such a shock," she managed. "One minute I was walking along, and the next minute it was around my neck." She shivered violently. "Oh, God, it was awful."

"The snake was probably as terrified as you," Alex comforted.

Dana took a few deep breaths and stepped away. She hadn't meant to cling to him. "It could have bitten me. Do you think it was poisonous?" The possibility made her ill.

"I have no idea. There're hundreds of snakes in Africa. No point in wondering now, anyway. It's long gone." He put two fingers under her chin and studied her face. "Are you going to be okay? Can you keep going?"

"Of course. I'm fine. I just had a momentary nervous breakdown." She gave him a weak smile.

"I thought you were the outdoor type, the rough-and-ready girl who wouldn't be afraid of snakes."

"I have a healthy respect for them," she said, "when they stay were they belong—on the ground. But flying snakes are another matter."

Alex laughed.

"Well, it was airborne when it landed on me!" She shivered again, thinking about the snake's sinuous coils. "Thanks for coming to the rescue. I was too frightened and surprised to do anything but scream."

"No problem. Now that you're all right, let's get going. And don't worry, I promise to keep a lookout for snakes." Alex stalked down the trail, and Dana followed, hating that she needed him. But she did, as they both knew. He'd made that point to her back at the tent, and while he hadn't mentioned it again, the fact of her dependency was implicit. The episode with the snake had just made it more obvious.

Confused and weary, Dana prayed that the day would soon end.

When sunset finally came, she welcomed it in one way and in another dreaded it. She was relieved to be able to sit down in front of the campfire with food and drink. But she hated thinking about the night to come when she would share the tent with Alex, lie next to him, wake beside him.

They made camp and ate in silence. Afterward, Dana cleaned up and finished preparing for bed while Alex put up the tent, a task that seemed to take on much greater importance than usual. She watched for a few minutes and then sat by the fire, arms on her knees, her head resting on her arms, lost in thought.

She jumped when Alex shook her shoulder. "Why don't you turn in for the night?"

"I'm trying to decide if I'd rather sleep in the tent with you or outside with the snakes. It's a hard choice. But then some people might say there's no difference."

She'd spoken without thinking, but Alex just grinned, unbothered, and sat down on the other side of the fire. He poured a cup of weak tea they'd brewed with the last tea bag. "Bitterness doesn't become you, Dana."

"I'm not bitter, but I am angry."

Alex sipped his tea. The firelight played over his face. He'd lost weight, she realized; the lines of his cheekbones were more prominently defined, and there were new creases in his forehead. He looked directly at her, meeting her gaze dead-on. "I made love to you because I wanted to, Dana. It had nothing to do with the elephant or Louis or anything that happened in Porte Ivoire or Brazzaville. It had everything to do with you and me."

What was the point of arguing? She didn't believe him; she certainly couldn't trust him. In a flat, neutral voice she said, "Since I can't change what happened, I might as well accept it. And live with it."

"Thanks for the compliment." His lips curved in a half smile. "I guess if you brought home a rogue like me, your brothers wouldn't approve."

"I told you once before, my brothers don't run my life." She didn't add that she couldn't imagine taking him home—with or without approval—a rogue, if not a murderer.

"But you care what they think."

"Of course I do. They're my family. Don't you care what your family thinks?"

"Don't have any."

Dana looked at him questioningly.

"I was an only child, and my parents are both dead now. Even if they were alive, I'd still be living my way."

Dana bristled at the comment. "I told you before, I'm also perfectly capable of living my life my way."

He shrugged, seemingly willing to end the conversation there, but she wouldn't let it drop. "Weren't you close to your parents?" When he didn't answer she decided to try another tack. "Maybe they never gave you the support you needed."

"Give it a rest, Dana."

"Why can't you talk about yourself?" she said. "What do you have to hide?"

He poked at the fire with a long stick. "You're an impossible woman, determined to go on and on."

He was right, but the more he tried to put her off, the more determined she became to know the real Alex Jourdan, to find out about his life. What drove the man? Why was he the way he was? No matter how she felt about him now, she couldn't rid herself of the fascination.

"There's one way to keep me from going on and on. Tell me about yourself, and I'll shut up."

Alex shook his head in frustration.

"What about your mother?"

"Beautiful, bright and demanding. She made a tremendous mistake when she married my father."

"That's a terrible thing to say."

"Aren't you the one who always insists on the truth?" he asked. "The truth is that my mother never should have married him. She was taking the grand tour of Europe after college, ready for romance and adventure. She met my father in Paris. He was handsome, charming and no match for her. So of course they fell in love."

He made the word *love* sound like something you caught, a bad cold or worse. "What did your father do for a living?"

"Not much of anything. He got by on his looks and his charisma. My mother tried to tame him, push him into a lucrative job. She decided on sales. He tried it, did okay, but never got serious. So when I was about five, they moved to New York. Even though she'd failed to make him into the man she wanted, they didn't know that back in the States. She was in her element with a French husband, more handsome than any movie star, and a kid who was very cute and very spoiled."

"And we know who," Dana commented.

"Yep. The world-traveler kid with the crazy parents. My father liked to keep moving, enjoy life, look for adventure. She wanted to settle down—in the lap of luxury, of course. I know what you're thinking—I got a little of both of them. But I'm more like one than the other."

Dana frowned.

"You'll see. Meanwhile, they went looking for a home. They looked in San Francisco, Denver, you name it, while the bills piled up. My father just didn't have it in him to make enough money to buy her happiness. That's when she got busy and found husband number two."

Dana was surprised. "What did your father do, go back to France?"

Alex finished his tea and stirred the coals again before he answered. "No, actually he...killed himself."

The remark came so suddenly that Dana had no time to prepare for it.

"He was a Frenchman, you see, and they're romantics if nothing else, always looking for the grand gesture. In reality, he couldn't face his failures." Alex's voice was bitter, and a look of sadness flitted briefly across his face, to be quickly replaced by his usual sardonic expression.

"Anyway," he went on, "by then my mother finally had struck gold in marriage number three. My last stepfather was a very rich man. I was ready to take whatever he had to offer even though I detested him. As soon as I finished school, I left. My mother died two years later, and I haven't seen my stepfather since. He didn't like me any more than I liked him."

Dana was quiet, listening to the only sounds around them, the sounds of the swamp—incessantly croaking frogs, squawking birds, the whisper of wind. She wished she knew what to say.

Alex spoke for her. "You don't need to draw any meaningful conclusions from what I've just told you, Dana. I understand myself perfectly. My father did everything for love, and my mother did everything for money. So while I have a little of his wanderlust, you may have guessed that I'm my mother's son."

"I don't believe—"

"But surely you do, Dana. If you can believe I'm a thief and a killer, you can easily believe that I'd do almost anything for money, big money, that is."

"Like your mother. But I wonder if that made her happy."

"I think so. She had no money of her own, but my stepfather indulged her totally. Her last years were lived in the lap of luxury. I don't want to wait until my last years. If money can't buy happiness, it's certainly convenient to have around."

"Even if it's illegally acquired?"

"Well, let's say on the fringes of the law. I was always eager to take advantage of my stepfather's name—without his permission, of course—which gave me entrée to wealthy people, many of them collectors."

"Of what?"

"Whatever money could buy. Don't look so shocked, Dana. I was never into drugs or flesh peddling. I dealt in antiquities—"

"Stolen?"

"I never asked. The Mediterranean provided a lucrative market for my—" he smiled ironically "—import-export business. I enjoyed being successful. I got sidetracked in Porte Ivoire for a while, but I plan to get back on top. It beats the way I grew up.''

Dana didn't answer. Instead, she got to her feet and headed for the tent. "You're right. I am tired, Alex. I'll see you in the morning."

MANY PEOPLE KNEW of the elephant. It was legendary, the stuff that dreams were made of. But only a handful knew that the Egyptian had it. Any other man would have come after the prize. Why hadn't he?

Maybe he had. Maybe the Egyptian was out there. That would make everything very complicated. Someone else would have to die.

Louis Bertrand had died for the prize. He hadn't been the first. Now, it seemed, he wouldn't be the last. Those who knew about the elephant would do anything to get it. The situation was becoming dangerous. It had to be ended. And soon.

SHE WOKE later than usual and crawled out of the tent feeling groggy and tired, limbs heavy, eyes bleary, her mind filled with Alex's confidences of the night before. She couldn't erase from her mind the picture of a little boy, unsettled, moving from town to town, torn by the love of his parents. And it *was* love, Dana realized. In his way, he'd loved the dreamer in both of his parents, even though theirs were very different dreams.

But the psychology behind Alex's offerings of the night before wasn't her concern now. Now she had to worry about her lethargy, wonder if she was coming down with malaria or some other disease. She had to worry about Alex's map and directions made in the Pygmy camp, which might be nothing more than squiggles. She had to worry about being on the trail again and encountering snakes and crocodiles, not to mention heat, insects and painful, pelting rainstorms.

Dana, who hated uncertainty, was faced with just that. Most importantly, she didn't know whether or not the man she slept next to, the man she had foolishly made love to, murdered his best friend. She had no idea what the next day, the next minute, would bring.

He'd promised to get her out alive, but his promises meant nothing.

Aware of that, she went out to face the morning—and Alex.

She found him withdrawn and quiet, staring moodily into the distance. Without comment, she began the usual breakfast preparations.

But there was nothing normal about today's ritual. Her anxieties were in full bloom, and she found herself jumping at every sound in the nearby swamp. She was trapped, not only by the swamp but by her own morass of foreboding and despair.

They were down to the last of the food; the tea and coffee were gone. That worried her, too. She wondered if Alex was any kind of a hunter. Somehow, she couldn't imagine him going out into the forest with his blowgun, bow and arrow or even pistol to catch game. If he couldn't find food for them, Dana imagined herself as provider, slogging through the swamp, gathering berries and roots for them to eat.

"They'd probably be poisonous and kill us both," she muttered aloud.

Suddenly, Alex sprang up and grabbed her, covering her mouth with his hand as he pulled her to her feet. He whispered hoarsely in her ear. "Someone is out there. Get into the tent and be quiet." He gave her a little shove. "Jean Luc's gun is in my bedroll. Use it if you have to."

If Dana knew one thing it was not to fight Alex when he made a demand like that. Obediently, she headed for the tent, looking back once to see Alex, his face tense, his gun drawn.

Once inside the tent, she scurried to the other side, as far away as possible. Still, she could hear someone approaching, footsteps furtive, cautious. There was the whisper of vines breaking, the snap of a twig underfoot. Could it be Kantana? Not so soon, she thought. But maybe, just maybe... If he was out there, would she really give herself up to him?

She didn't know.

Hunched in the corner of the tent, Dana held her breath and waited. Silence. Nothing happened. But something was going to occur—soon; they couldn't avoid it now. There was no place to hide.

She found the gun and held it helplessly in her hand. She'd shot rifles in target practice with her brothers, but she'd never used a handgun. Keeping the muzzle pointed to the ground, she gathered up the necessary strength, mental and physical, to creep to the entrance, pull back the flap an inch or two and peer out. Alex was waiting in the shadow of a tree, his gun raised and steady.

All kinds of dramatic scenarios played wildly in her head. Alex shooting Kantana, plunging them even deeper into trouble, cop killers on the run for the rest of their lives. Or Kantana killing Alex, leaving Dana prisoner again, behind bars forever in the Porte Ivoire jail.

But what if it wasn't Kantana? What if it was the mysterious killer of Alex's hypothesis? Dana closed the flap. Kantana was a threat, but he wouldn't kill her unless she ran from him—and maybe not even then. But she couldn't predict her fate at the hands of Louis's hypothetical murderer. A person who'd killed once wouldn't hesitate to do it again.

There was a third, even more frightening possibility. The man who last owned the elephant could have sent a band of mercenaries to reclaim it. That thought caused perspiration to break out on Dana's forehead. It was the worst scenario. Against mercenaries, they didn't have a chance.

There was one answer to each of those possibilities—the Elephant d'Or. Give it to them!

Frantically, Dana rummaged through Alex's backpack, checking all the hiding places, but she couldn't find the elephant. Where had he hidden it? Why hadn't she paid attention? She needed it desperately for them to get out of this situation alive. She would willingly hand it over to anyone in return for their lives...Alex's greed be damned!

There was a sudden rustle in the bushes at the edge of the camp. Dana heard it, and the click as Alex cocked his pistol. Even in her fear, she found herself creeping to the front of the tent, her heart fluttering wildly in her chest.

The footsteps stopped. The silence that followed was unnerving. It grew and grew until Dana wanted to scream. Instead, she remained perfectly still, trying to ignore the cramps that were beginning in her calves. Mosquitoes and insects buzzed incessantly around her. The perspiration continued down her face and neck into the valley between her breasts. Tension mounted, vibrated on the hot, moist air like a living thing.

Then she heard the movement again, rustling from the brush. She tensed, grasping the gun in her sweaty palm as a large man, holding his hands above his head, burst into the camp.

"Don't shoot, mate. It's me. Mac McQuire. How's about a cuppa tea with a little shot of whiskey to start the day?"

Chapter Ten

Alex didn't lower his gun. "What the hell are you doing here, Mac?"

"Please, mate, the gun makes me nervous."

"Answer my question," Alex said through clenched teeth.

"I will, just as soon as you put the gun away and give a pal a drink."

"We're out of everything," Alex said flatly. "Except water, and that's getting low."

"Water I have plenty of," Mac replied, tossing his canteen on the ground. "It's yours. Now the gun, mate."

Alex shoved the gun into his belt, well aware that the Irishman wasn't going to try anything in broad daylight. Mac was a sneakier sort. "I'm ready for your explanation."

"Simple, mate. Been tracking the Pygmies to do a little trading. Imagine my surprise when I came upon two other sets of footprints, definitely not our barefooted little Mgembe." He grinned broadly. "Being the curious type, when the tribe took off after the elephant, I decided to find out where the other two chaps went. Who's your partner?"

"Come on out and meet my friend," Alex called to Dana, hoping she would put the gun back in the bedroll. No point in giving away everything to Mac.

When she slipped out of the tent empty-handed, Alex breathed a sigh of relief—until he saw the look McQuire gave her. The Irishman's eyes ate her up, and Alex realized why. Even with her wrinkled clothes, hair pulled back and no makeup, Dana was a hell of a good-looking woman. Her blue eyes seemed huge against her recently acquired tan, and because she'd lost weight, her features seemed more finely chiseled. Mac was probably thinking that she looked almost fragile; Alex knew that Dana Baldwin was anything but dainty.

In fact, she was something pretty exciting to come upon in the middle of the jungle, for any man. And from the look in Mac's eyes, Alex saw trouble brewing. Besides the swamp, the dwindling supplies, the race against time, he now had another problem. Mac McQuire was lusting after Dana.

"Mac, this is Dana," he said matter-of-factly. No need for explanation, Alex thought as he watched Mac's next move. The Irishman bent over Dana's hand, bringing it to his lips and spouting an abundance of Gaelic superlatives in response to her beauty.

Alex interrupted. "No time for speeches, Mac. We're moving on."

"Surely, you have time for a cuppa tea." He swung his pack to the ground and reached inside. "Yes, mate, I have the tea, and a bit of whiskey to make it palatable."

"Alex, please, I'd love some tea," Dana pleaded. "And maybe your friend can help us."

"Maybe I can. Just maybe," Mac said as he built up the fire, adding twigs and boiling the water.

"My *friend* has helped us enough," Alex snapped. "He was the one who told Kantana we escaped up-river."

Mac looked up, squinting into the sun. "That was before I knew the problem. If you'd told me you were on the run, I would've lied for you."

Alex didn't believe that, but he kept quiet, waiting and wondering. Maybe it was time to give Mac a little leeway and find out what kind of game he was playing.

"And if I'd met the lass, why, the good Lord knows what lengths I would've gone to in order to protect the two of you. Anyone with eyes in his head can see at first glance that the lady isn't capable of committing murder."

Dana smiled gratefully at Mac and then scowled at Alex, who forced himself to hold off before chasing the damned Irishman away. While he tried to be patient, he couldn't help being irritated that she seemed taken with Mac.

"What's your last name, my lass?" Mac asked.

"Baldwin," Dana answered, accepting a cup of strong tea but refusing the whiskey.

"Ah, yes. Baldwin. I know that name. More than thirty years ago, I took a man called Baldwin into the rain forest...."

So that was it, Alex thought. He figured Mac had something up his sleeve. Now he knew what it was. The Irishman had done a little research and made a surprise discovery, which he was going to milk for all it was worth. Alex watched him ingratiate himself to Dana.

Mac's revelation had left her speechless, giving the Irishman a chance to inquire, "Could that man have been your father?"

Alex rolled his eyes heavenward as Dana answered, "Yes, oh, yes! I'd love to talk to you about my father and the trip. I have all his notes, but—"

That was enough, Alex decided. "Maybe Mac can write you a letter about it, Dana, but now we don't have time. We're running late as it is."

While Dana seethed, Mac took the pot off the fire and said to Alex, "Maybe you have more time than you think. Kantana's not on your trail." He offered Alex a cup of tea, and the refusal didn't seem to bother the Irishman, who poured a cup for himself and added a little whiskey.

"What are you talking about, Mac?"

"Seems the little lady here dislocated Kantana's shoulder during what I hear was quite a tussle. He had to go downriver to have it set, and no one in Port Ivoire is organized enough to set up a search party," Mac added with a chuckle.

"Then we can relax a little," Dana said, "and you can tell me about your time with my father."

"Sure, I'd like to do that—"

"No," Alex said definitely. "We're not slowing down." They had a rendezvous across the border, and they had to get there within the agreed time frame to meet the plane. The clock was ticking.

Mac's eyes had a foxy, curious look. "You're meeting someone, perhaps?"

Alex frowned at Dana, warning her to keep quiet. "My mission is to get the lady safely out of the Congo. Even though you're right about one thing, that Dana is innocent of murder, Jean Luc doesn't know that. Besides, she broke out of jail and assaulted an officer." He ignored Dana's look of contempt at his lie. "You found us easily. Others could do the same. So we're moving on."

Alex kicked dirt over the fire, from which Mac barely retrieved his teapot in time.

Mac kept his smile intact as he responded to Alex. "Sure I found you, but it wasn't that easy, my mate. I came upriver looking for the Pygmy..."

Alex paid no attention to Mac as he quickly took down the tent and motioned for Dana to gather their supplies, which she did grudgingly.

Mac packed up his canteen and teapot without losing a beat in his story. "I thought the Mgembe might have some ivory we could negotiate on. Then I found your tracks heading for the swamp. I thought maybe I should come on along and warn you."

"Warn us?" Dana stopped packing and looked up at him. "What more could there be? We've encountered crocs and hippos and snakes, we've heard about the monster that the Pygmies are so afraid of...what more should we be worried about in this hellhole?"

"Quicksand. Lots of it when you get nearer the river, and I'm guessing you plan to ford Bonsuko River to get across the border."

"Quicksand?" Dana turned to Alex. "Did you know about that?"

He shouldered his pack. "It's marked on my map. Now let's get going."

"It might be on your map, my pal, but I have it here, in my head," the Irishman said, giving the side of his brow a pat. "I can lead you right through the sand like a leprechaun through the Irish bogs."

"The question is, why the hell would you do that for us, McQuire?" Alex cut in coldly, worried that he knew the reason—Mac had heard about the Elephant d'Or.

"Why, you ask? I answer, why not?" Mac's reply was affable. "Life along the Lomami can be dull, but escorting a lady, especially one who is fleeing a charge of murder—" He smiled widely at Dana and made a low, courtly bow. "Not that I believe it. Let's just say that it would be an honor to guide you through the swamp. Your father was one of the first to hire me when I started my business, and Mac McQuire never forgets a favor."

Mac's words were said on the run as he hurried after Alex, already on the trail and pulling Dana along with him.

ALEX WAS A PAIN all day and well into the night, as far as Dana was concerned, never taking his eyes off Mac. He didn't even seemed impressed, and certainly wasn't grateful, that Mac had pointed out the quicksand bogs and cleverly helped them avoid trouble.

But Dana was pleased to have his company. And what really intrigued her was that Mac remembered her father so well. Their talk over dinner at the campfire had been revealing, nostalgic and insightful. It brought back wonderful memories. And Mac seemed just as interested in the Mgembe as she, and much more knowledgeable. All that was in his favor.

Then why did Alex mistrust the man? Why did he stay awake long after Mac began snoring away by the campfire? Alex didn't trust him; she didn't trust Alex.

Dana tried to put that doubt out of her head as she drifted off to sleep. But when she woke suddenly, an hour or so later, Alex was more alert than ever.

"Alex—"

"Quiet," he ordered. "Mac is moving around out there, and I'm not going to sleep until I'm sure that he's no longer a threat."

"He seems all right to me."

"He's a stranger, Dana. You don't know him."

But I know you, she thought. Aloud she said sharply, "I'm too tired to argue. Stay up and watch him all night if you want to." She rolled over in her sleeping bag, deliberately turning her back on him.

An hour before dawn, she opened her eyes to find the jungle quiet and Alex asleep beside her. She had an overwhelming urge to take charge of her own destiny.

Dana didn't share Alex's suspicions of Mac, who was nothing more than a professional guide. And the fact that he had taken her father through the jungle, that gave them a special bond. From what she'd seen of Mac the day before, he was a hell of a good guide. She had confidence that he could get her across the border into Zaire. With Alex, she still didn't know what to expect.

She reached for her shoes. She could wake Mac and bribe him to take her across the border. Then what? She considered her predicament. Mac was a risk, but with him she'd be free—and free of her entanglement with Alex. Wasn't that what she wanted?

As if in answer to her question, she pushed back the flap and slipped into the warm Congo air.

Dana walked a few yards into the brush where she'd created her bathroom, and afterward returned to the camp slowly, quietly, being careful not to disturb any sleeping creatures. She'd seen enough of the jungle's dangers to last her a lifetime.

While she was considering what to do about Mac, she realized that he'd made the decision for her. Ahead, near the campfire, she saw a movement, a shadowy figure that could only be the guide. She smiled and moved toward him. Now she could feel him out, discover how he really felt about Alex and find out if he'd be interested in taking her across the border. Alone.

Dana walked toward him, her footsteps muffled on the sandy soil. Then she saw what he was doing. Alex had left a pack out in the open near the fire, and Mac was methodically rifling through it!

She turned away, hoping to get to the tent before he saw her. But it was too late. One long stride and he was beside her, the blade of his knife gleaming sharply in the moonlight. His fingers wrapped around her upper arm like a vise. She didn't have a chance to scream before he pressed the knife against her neck.

"I was hoping to find it and get the hell out."

"The elephant," she said sadly. Nothing could surprise her now.

"Right-o, my lassie. The golden elephant." He tossed the pack aside. "I should have known Alex would set a trap, leaving this pack out in the open. But I had to look."

Dana felt her legs go weak, her head spin. There was no one to trust now.

He didn't let her fall. "Don't you go fainting on me. You're the one I'm counting on to tell me where the elephant's hidden."

Dana felt the cold, sharp edge of the knife against her skin. She was paralyzed with fear, fear of this man who had been so kind to her, who had been her father's guide and seemingly his friend, and now Mac was her captor. She had nowhere to turn.

"Where is it?" he insisted.

"I've only seen the elephant once. I don't know where it is now."

Mac slid the knife along her neck to her chin. "You wouldn't be lying to me, would you? You and Alex look pretty cozy sharing that tent."

"A tent is all we share, not a bed. And I'm not lying. I wish you'd found the damned elephant. I wish it was a thousand miles from here. Let me go. Please." But if he released her what would she do—run into the swamp, or go back to Alex? All the possibilities seemed hopeless to her. "I don't know where it is," she repeated in a strained voice.

Mac sighed deeply. "Then it looks like Alex is going to have to tell me." He tightened his grip on Dana and called out in a booming voice, "Jourdan, get out here. I've got your woman!"

Dana saw Alex before Mac did. He was already out of the tent, in the shadows, his gun leveled at the Irishman. When Mac spotted him, he whirled around, keeping his hold on Dana. "Don't shoot," he called out as Alex tried to get a fix on him with the gun, "or you'll hit the woman."

Alex froze, the weapon still in his hand.

"Drop it," Mac cried. When Alex didn't comply, he grabbed Dana by her hair and pulled her head back. Then with the razor-sharp point of the knife he nicked the soft flesh under her chin.

She felt a stab of pain and cried out, but Mac just held her tighter.

"I could kill her in an instant," he called to Alex, "but I might not. Maybe I'll just scar up this pretty face a bit."

Dana moaned. She felt the warm blood drip down her neck. The instant of pain had passed, leaving only a numbing fear. She wanted to call to Alex, beg him to do as Mac ordered, but she couldn't find her voice, and

Alex still held the gun pointed at them. A horrible sensation swept over her, and for a long moment she thought he was going to shoot, kill them both. What did he care? He had the elephant.

Dana held her breath, waiting for Alex to make up his mind whether to shoot them or drop the gun.

"You have three seconds, pal," Mac said. "One—"

Alex lowered the gun.

"Good man. Now drop it."

Alex let the gun slide from his fingers to the soft bed of the jungle floor, and Dana breathed again.

"Now let Dana go," Alex said. "She's the innocent in all this, Mac. She knows nothing."

Mac's laughter rumbled low in his chest. "No one involved with you is ever innocent, pal. Now tell me where the elephant is—or your lovely lady friend will be minus a nose." Mac slid the flat side of his knife along her chin, and Dana gave a barely audible moan.

"It's about a mile from here, into the swamp."

"And just how did it get there?" The knife turned slightly in his hand, its blade creasing her cheek.

"I knew you were after it, so I hid it last night. I'll take you there," Alex offered, "but first tell me how you figure in this."

"I was hired," Mac offered in a friendly voice.

"I'm not very patient this morning," Alex said. "So let's get to the point. Who hired you?"

"An old friend of yours, Maurice Longongo."

Alex let out a quick breath. "The son of a bitch."

Dana finally had the courage to speak. "You always suspected him, Alex."

Alex nodded. "He was at the party, he knew the elephant was missing and he followed Louis—"

"And murdered him," Dana said, feeling a sudden relief that it wasn't Alex after all.

"And when he realized that you and I had the elephant—"

This time Mac completed Alex's thought. "He hired me to come after you. Longongo is out there, too, somewhere in the bush with his porters and bearers. Traveling in style."

Alex frowned. "Civil servants don't make that kind of money."

Mac lowered his knife and relaxed his hold on Dana without letting her go. "The Egyptian is bankrolling him. You must know that a man that ruthless wouldn't let his prize go so easily."

Alex smiled ruefully. "Obviously, I'm not as good at this cat-and-mouse game as I thought."

"Which is why I'm taking over. The sun will be up in a few minutes. I want the elephant. Now."

Dana drew a long breath of relief. Everything was going to work out. Alex would give Mac the elephant, Mac would get the hell away from them and they could continue on their journey—unless Alex decided to get the elephant back.

The cat-and-mouse game could go on forever, but Dana didn't want to worry about that now, especially when she knew at last that Alex wasn't a killer. It had been Longongo all along. Something good had come of this part of their journey. They'd learned the truth.

But Alex hadn't moved. Dana groaned inwardly when she saw his adamant stance. Her nerves were so tightly strung that at any second she felt she might snap. Why was Alex delaying like this? Each minute was a torturous hour for her.

"Let's go, Jourdan," Mac ordered.

"Just one question," Alex said. "After I give you the elephant, what's stopping you from killing us and heading for the border on your own, forgetting about Longongo and the Egyptian?"

"The Egyptian has long arms, mate."

"And the elephant is worth a small fortune," Alex replied.

"Now don't be putting ideas in my head. I'm just a simple guide, doing what I'm paid to do."

At that moment Dana knew that Mac was going to kill them, as surely as if he'd said the words. It was in the coldness of his voice, his total lack of humanity.

Somehow, she realized that Alex had wanted her to know. But why, just so she could suffer even more? That wasn't possible and—she knew now—it wasn't like Alex. There was another reason, if she could just discover what it was! Confusion mixed with fear inside of Dana. She didn't know how much more she could stand.

THEY PACKED UP and headed into the bowels of the swamp. Dana felt as if they were treading on dynamite. Every step Alex took was measured and careful, and Mac and Dana followed tentatively in his footsteps as he moved from hummock to hummock, testing each section of firm ground before making another move. All around them the quicksand bogs lay steaming in the sun, their shining surfaces innocent looking, belying the sinister depths below where one misstep could mean an agonizing death.

The air was hot and still. Unrelenting mosquitoes and huge flies buzzed hungrily around their faces. Dana dared not move her hand to slap them away for fear the movement might cause Mac to respond violently. Perspiration ran down her face and puddled between her breasts. She wanted to scream and run in terror; instead she stayed by Mac's side as they inched along behind Alex.

She saw his foot slip into the powerful, sucking sand and almost called out. But Alex caught himself and braced against a tree to keep from tumbling off the trail into the quicksand. Still, it took a powerful effort to pull his leg out.

There was fear in Mac's voice as he lashed out at Alex. "Where the hell are you taking us? Even I don't know this part of the swamp. If you're planning some kind of trick—"

"I didn't slip on purpose, Mac, believe me," Alex said as he found solid footing and wiped his sweating face with his forearm. "This place can trick a man. I thought I remembered the tree that was my landmark, but—"

"You damn well better remember," Mac growled.

Alex narrowed his eyes against the sun. "I see it—that dead tree ahead that looks like a skeleton's arm. Not much farther."

He set out confidently, much too sure, Dana thought as she picked her way carefully behind, trying to keep in his footsteps. Mac was pushing her on, but she refused to be hurried when death lay just a few feet away on either side of the trail.

"Get a move on, woman," Mac said.

But Dana could only creep along at a snail's pace, fearful of a misstep.

"Faster," Mac insisted. "He's getting too far ahead."

Alex was widening the gap between them when Dana heard his cry and saw him sliding feet first into the shimmering bog.

"Oh, my God! Alex!" She began to run, stumbling toward him, forgetful of the dangerous sands all around, forgetful of Mac, who forged after her, cursing.

Alex was a prisoner of the quicksand, fighting to stay upright as it crept around his waist. Dana flung herself onto the ground and grabbed his hand. She screamed at Mac. "Get the other hand, pull him out!" Hysterical with fear, she watched as Alex was pulled down, steadily, quickly, right in front of her. She couldn't bear it. All her conflicting feelings about him surged into one overwhelming emotion—fear that she might lose him forever.

"Help him, please help him," she cried.

Mac stood stoically above them, measuring Alex with his cold eyes. "Where's the elephant?"

"For God's sake, Mac," Dana cried. "He's going under!"

Mac didn't move. "Tell me," he insisted.

"Pull me out," Alex replied.

"Stop it!" Dana screamed. "This isn't the time for a battle of wills." She held onto Alex's hand, which was slippery in her grasp.

"You'll never find the elephant, Mac. I'd have to draw a map, and that would be a little difficult, considering—"

"Tell me!" Mac insisted.

"Dammit, man, don't you understand? I can barely remember how to get there myself. Now pull me out of this bog, and I'll take you to it. That's our only chance. Otherwise I die, and you'll never see the elephant."

Mac swore violently before reaching down for Alex's free hand.

"Dana, get out of the way," Alex ordered. "Mac's strong enough to pull me out of here on his own. Remember Kantana!" he cried out, as if the words were some kind of call to action.

And they were! Dana realized it immediately. He wanted her to remember how she handled Kantana, running into the camp and taking him by surprise.

As Mac grabbed for Alex's hands, she saw the powerful muscles of the guide's body tense, saw Alex reach up toward him. Just as the men's hands touched, she flung herself at Mac, hitting him squarely in the back. At the same moment, Alex grabbed his hands and pulled.

Mac sailed over Alex into the quicksand, hitting the surface headfirst, driven deeply into the swamp by his forward momentum.

"Oh, God!" Dana screamed. "What can we do?"

Her cries reverberated through the swamp as Mac struggled frantically to right himself. But his nose and mouth had filled with sand, and he never had a chance to breathe. All she could do was watch, horrified, as the greedy ooze sucked him down, squeezing the breath—and life—from him.

"Close your eyes," Alex shouted. "Don't watch. There's nothing you can do."

She turned away, covering her face with her hands, but she couldn't shut out the sound of the bog claiming its victim, the slurping, gurgling sound of death.

Finally she heard Alex's voice. "He's gone, Dana. It's over, and it was quick."

She turned and dropped to her knees at the edge of the bog, holding out her hands to Alex again.

"You're not strong enough to get me out, Dana. It's hopeless." He clung with one hand to the root of a tree, but the bog oozed upward to his chest. "I want you to go now, take the elephant and try to make it across the border."

"No!" Dana cried out in frustration and rage. "Listen you fool, I don't care about the elephant. I care about you, and I'm not letting you leave me, not when I finally know what I always believed was true—you're not a murderer," she cried. "I believed that all along, and now I'll never let you go. Hold on, dammit," she demanded, stretching out her hands toward him again.

"This is no good, Dana," Alex said as he slipped farther into the bog.

"There must be something, some way," she cried in frustration.

"You could never pull me out of here. We need leverage." He looked around frantically. "If only— I know! In the duffel bag, there's rope—"

Dana didn't wait for him to finish. She grabbed the bag, rummaged through and found it.

"Can you make a lasso?"

She had already begun the knot. "I'm from Colorado, remember?" She completed the loop and stood up.

"Toss it to me, carefully."

Dana had a better idea. "Hold your arms above your head," she told him as she twirled the rope twice in the air and then sailed it toward him. The lasso settled lazily over his head.

"I didn't know you were a cowgirl," Alex said as he secured it around his chest.

"There's a great deal you don't know." Dana wrapped the rope around a tree at the edge of the bog, braced her feet against solid ground and began to pull. Slowly Alex walked his hands along the rope. It was a grueling, inch-by-inch process, but they'd found the answer, and Dana knew that all she needed was enough resilience to keep pulling until he was free. She wound the rope once around her wrists and summoned up her strength for what lay ahead.

IT SEEMED LIKE HOURS later when a panting, exhausted Alex pulled himself onto dry land, collapsing beside Dana, who wrapped her arms around him. He was wet and filthy—but alive. She drew his face to hers and kissed him hungrily, holding on to him with all her might, as if she feared losing him again to the swamp.

He tasted her tears as they kissed; he felt her tremble in his arms. Protectively, he gathered her closer.

"You idiot," she chided between kisses. "You took such a chance going into that quicksand."

"He was going to kill us and take off with the elephant. I had to do something to save myself—and you. I would never let anything happen to you." He kissed her again, laughing at the picture they created, two dirty, bedraggled figures lying in each others' arms in the depths of the sweltering swamp.

"Well, you didn't have to nearly die to make your point," Dana said, still holding tightly.

"That was a mistake," he replied with a grin. "I meant to slip in at the edge of the bog and make it look like the quicksand had me. I went a little too far."

"I'll say."

"But you saved me," he told her, kissing her muddy face. "You're quite a woman. Remind me to take you along next time I go into a swamp."

"I wouldn't travel with anyone else," she said, looking at him through tears of joy. "And I never thought you were a killer, Alex. Not deep in my heart."

"You could have fooled me."

"Well, things looked pretty bad for you."

"I recall a moment there when they didn't look so good for you," Alex reminded her.

"Did you really think I killed Louis?"

"The thought crossed my mind, but you're not a killer, either, Dana."

"What about Mac? I killed him, Alex." Shivering, she hid her face against his chest.

"We both did, Dana. We had no choice." He held her close as she began to cry. He felt a tremendous wave of tenderness wash over him. Awkwardly, he patted her hair. "It's all right, baby. We're going to make it. We're going to be okay."

She raised her tearstained face. "I'm so tired, Alex. I can't keep going."

"Yes, you can. The old mission is on the other side of the river. Just a few more miles. We can do it, Dana."

"No, I can't. I'm—"

He kissed her gently on the lips. "Yes, you can. Together we can do anything."

"But we have to find the damned elephant, and—"

Alex began to laugh.

"What's so funny?"

"The elephant's in the duffel bag."

ALEX JOURDAN would have to die. It was the only way. He wouldn't hand over the elephant without a fight. Even if he was subdued and the prize stolen, he'd take his revenge on the person who took it from him.

And then there was Dana. She was the kind who'd have no hesitation about calling the authorities, alerting Interpol, insisting that the elephant end up in some damned museum. In her way, she was as dangerous as Alex.

It would be just as easy to kill them both and leave their bodies to rot in the hot African sun.

Chapter Eleven

"I see the mission, Dana. Just over that rise."

Alex pulled her along toward their destination. Just one more obstacle, she thought, following an interminable morning when they'd crossed the final swamp bog and forded the Bonsuko River. She held on to Alex's arm with both hands as he all but carried her over the final slope to the remains of the old Catholic mission.

Once inside its crumbling walls, Dana collapsed on the ground, struggling to breathe evenly, trying to relax in spite of the fierce pain in her side and the cramps in her legs. "I'll never walk normally again," she said.

Alex pulled her into his arms. "You can lean on me," he said softly.

"I've been leaning on you most of the day. Thanks for getting me here, Alex."

He smiled at her. "Thanks for saving my life." He kissed her on the forehead. "Soon we'll be out of here."

She looked around. "I suppose your pilot can find the place easy enough from the air. But is there room for a plane to land?"

"Glenn's an old bush pilot. He can put her down almost anywhere."

"You're frowning," Dana noted. "Does that mean you're worried, too?"

Alex got up after gently extricating himself from her tired arms and letting her lean back against a partial wall. He walked around the building and surveyed the surrounding area. "There's a clearing over there. Come and see."

Dana moaned. "Why don't you tell me about it? I can't move."

"Two clearings, actually, this lower one and a plateau on the other side, with a deep gorge in between."

"Oh, great. The plane can fall in!"

Alex laughed. "It was on the map. And a swinging bridge connects the flatlands and the plateau, just as the Pygmies told you. That gives us a natural landing strip on either side with plenty of room to put the plane down. We've got it made, Dana."

"Just so he lands on *this* side. I'm not much in the mood to cross the Pygmy bridge!"

"Don't worry. The mission is our landmark." Alex came back and sat down beside her. "Glenn will be here. Next stop, civilization and the city of Nairobi."

Dana sighed and leaned against him, so happy to feel comfortable again at his side, wondering what was in store for them in Nairobi. "What will you do then?" she asked, not including herself.

"Bathe. Shave. Eat. Sleep. And after that—" He gave her a sly look. "I expect to go out on the town with my partner."

"If I can walk."

"We'll take a cab. To the best restaurant in town where we'll eat rich food, drink mellow wines, dance exotic dances—"

"My legs—"

"I'll hold you up. And we'll kiss right on the dance floor and not care who sees—" A distant whirring noise interrupted him. "What's that?"

"The plane?" she asked.

Alex shook his head. "Sounds more like a helicopter." He stood up, and she struggled to her feet beside him, shielding her eyes against the sun.

"It could still be him—couldn't it?"

"Glenn's a bush pilot. He doesn't fly helicopters." Alex watched it approach. "Could be the police."

The noise got louder and louder, ear shattering when it hovered overhead.

"He's landing," Alex said as he grabbed her arm and pulled her into the shadow of the crumbling walls.

"Even if it's the police, let's go with them, Alex. We're in Zaire. Kantana can't get us here."

But Alex wasn't listening; he was watching the chopper as it came down in a swirl of sand and dust. Dana huddled beside him, hands over her ears, eyes closed. The rapid whirring noise turned into a slow whoosh as Dana crouched behind the wall, watching for a sign of life.

"Congo Waterways," Alex read the name on the chopper. "It's the touring company's chopper. What the hell are they—"

"They've come to rescue us, to get us out of here," Dana cried, without stopping to think. "Look!" A large, middle-aged woman dressed in khaki emerged from the hatch. With a glad cry, Dana scrambled over the wall and toward her. "Millie! Millie, am I glad to see you!"

Midway in her wild run, she caught sight of someone else getting out of the chopper behind Millie. It was

Yassif! Dana stopped in midstride, and at that moment Alex hit her from behind and fell on top of her.

They rolled over together in the dust, and then, half-crawling, Alex pulled Dana behind a section of wall, his hand on the back of her head, pushing it down. "Don't look up," he told her. "Yassif has a gun. Some kind of semiautomatic. He can blast us to mincemeat."

Dana struggled to get her breath. "Why would he shoot at us?" she cried.

The answer was a barrage of bullets over their heads.

Dana covered her ears and screamed. When the noise abated, she raised her head no more than an inch and shouted at Millie. "What the hell is going on? Are you insane? You should be helping us, not trying to kill us. What do you want?" Dana cried out in desperation.

"The elephant," Alex said. "She wants the damned elephant."

"Right, dear boy. Now hand it over."

Yassif punctuated the demand with another strafing from his gun.

Alex pushed Dana down flat into the dirt, cursed profanely under his breath and pulled his gun out.

"What good is that going to do against his weapon?" Dana asked. "All they have to do is kill us and take the elephant. We have nothing to negotiate with."

"But if you can keep her talking, maybe I can get around behind him."

"Alex—"

"It's our only chance."

Dana's head was swimming. She couldn't believe anything that had happened. "But Millie is my friend. She's—"

"A nut case who's joined forces with a madman," Alex told her. "Take my word for it. She'll probably tell you herself if you can get her talking. I'm depending on you—again,'' he whispered as he began to inch along the wall.

They had nothing to lose now. She was as willing as Alex to gamble on Lady Luck one more time. Somehow, she wasn't even afraid.

"All right, Millie," she called out in her loudest voice. "You can have the elephant. I hate it anyway. It's brought me nothing but bad luck, and it'll bring you the same."

"Never! It will buy me everything I need," Millie shouted. "I had as much right to it as Louis!"

"Millie, you didn't kill him!"

"Why not? I saw him steal the elephant. He had what I wanted, and I knew how to use a blowgun!"

"And you let me take the blame?" Dana crouched behind the wall, anger replacing her earlier confidence.

"You were a stranger and everyone wanted to believe you were guilty. That part was easy."

Dana remained hunched up, trying not to believe what she was hearing, while Alex crept with unbearable slowness along the wall.

"What about Yassif?" she managed to ask.

"He might not know much English, but he knows a great deal about choppers and guns. And the dear boy can read a map. He figured out you'd head here. It's a known meeting place for smugglers and criminals."

"But Betty—"

Millie's laugh was shrill. "The golden elephant was much more interesting to him than Betty, believe me," she said, snickering.

Yassif let go with another round of bullets that scarred the earth in front of Dana.

"He's getting trigger-happy, darling. You better give us the elephant."

"Millie, wait—"

Dana couldn't stall much longer, and she sensed that Millie knew it.

"Yassif's had enough, dearie. And frankly, so have I. Give me the elephant and he'll put away the gun."

Dana knew better. Yassif wouldn't put down his gun until she and Alex lay bleeding to death under the hot African sun. As for Millie, she'd killed Louis in cold blood—and he was her friend! Dana shuddered to think how easily she would kill a mere acquaintance—or direct Yassif to do it for her.

She looked frantically toward Alex, her heart in her throat. At that moment he reached the end of the wall where he stood up, threw a rock into the dirt behind the helicopter and ducked down so quickly she hardly saw it happen.

As Yassif turned toward the sound, his gun blazing, Alex began to shoot from behind the rock.

Dana huddled against the wall, waiting for the end of the battle, waiting for the silence that never came. Instead, the earth began to rumble and vibrate.

Forgetting the danger, she opened her eyes and looked over the rim of the wall as a shrill, maddened trumpeting filled the jungle.

She saw the elephants coming. So did Millie and Yassif, who raced for their chopper. For one horrifying instant, Dana watched their hopeless race against thousands of tons of enraged and frightened animals.

Alex was beside her instantly. "It's the elephant hunt! The Pygmies are driving the whole herd this way," Alex shouted.

Dana knew that the elephants would crush the helicopter—and its passengers—like popcorn.

Alex grabbed her hand. "We're taking the bridge. The last I heard, elephants can't fly."

Dana stumbled beside him, across the rocky soil toward the trees that edged the ravine. Behind them, she heard a hideous crunching as the elephants plowed into the chopper. Even above the trumpeting and pounding, she could hear the last dreadful screams of Millie and Yassif. And then silence. She didn't look back.

The rampaging elephants stopped for a moment, as if regrouping, and then turned and headed toward Alex and Dana, trampling everything in their path, filling the air with dust and shaking the earth with their deadly power.

"Get on the bridge, Dana," Alex yelled.

She took one look at the flimsy and insubstantial vine bridge stretched across the chasm. Maybe it could hold a Pygmy, but their combined weight was too much.

She balked.

Alex shoved her hard. "Get going. Now!"

Dana took her first shaky step, urged on by his command and the maddened trumpeting of the elephants.

ALEX KNEW as well as Dana that the vine bridge wasn't made for people their size. It was little more than a swing, constructed from twisted vines and grasses into rope and strung from one side of the ravine to the other. The Pygmies—moving rapidly, one at a time—could cross it easily. Two normal-size people—trudging carefully, holding onto the handrails that were much too low for them—were another matter.

In front of him, Dana tottered dangerously.

"Crouch down," he commanded. "Crawl toward the other side. It'll be okay if you just keep moving."

He saw her drop to her knees and begin to crawl, inching along the swaying, insubstantial bridge. He crawled behind her, urging her on. Only another fifteen or twenty feet and they were safe.

Suddenly there was a give in the bridge, a sickening sound as the vines began to pull away from their moorings.

"Alex, what's happening?" she called to him.

"Don't stop," he yelled. "Go for the other side!"

But before the words were out of his mouth, the bridge broke loose from the trees on the mission side of the ravine and with a sickening lurch hurtled toward the opposite wall.

"Hold on, hold on," he cried out.

They had only seconds to brace themselves against the jolting crash. It threw them into the dense brush that clung to the sides of the ravine.

Alex looked up and saw Dana, six feet above him, clinging desperately to the bridge that had become a tangled mass of vines. He was relieved to hear her call to him in a voice that was shaky but determined. "I guess all I have to do now is climb up."

"At least we're not swaying anymore," he yelled. "Give it a try, Dana."

He watched as she gingerly attempted to establish a foothold and shift her weight from one side of the vine to the other. It was a great effort but useless because the vines weren't holding, and she knew it. He watched her hang on grimly, suspended like a puppet on delicate, fragile strings. If he didn't do something quickly, both of them would end up on the bottom of the ravine.

"Hang on, Dana," he shouted.

"It's slipping, Alex. Oh, God, it's slipping," she called to him.

"Don't worry, it'll support you. I'm letting go."

"No, Alex—"

"Dana, what's left of the bridge won't hold both of us. It's going to break any minute. There's a narrow ledge about ten feet below. I'm going to drop down to it."

"Don't you dare let go! Don't you leave me!"

"The vines will support you, and when I let go, you can make it to the top."

"No!"

"Dana, listen to me. One of us has to flag down Glenn. He won't land if no one's there," Alex insisted. "I'll try to let go gently, but there might be some swaying so hold on."

"Alex—"

"Hold on, Dana. I'm dropping onto the ledge now."

She cried out to him again, but he had already pushed away from the wall. She felt the vines swing out and then go slack. Seconds later, she heard the sound of his body crashing through branches and bushes. Then there was one last horrific thud.

"Alex, are you all right? Alex!" she screamed.

There was no response. Dana looked down. Branches had broken from the trees as he crashed by, but she still couldn't see all the way to the ledge. There was nothing but green visible below her. And in the distance she could hear the sound of the elephants rampaging on the other side of the ravine.

Fighting back her sobs, Dana began to pull herself toward the top of the chasm. It was slow going as she found a foothold and eased her body another inch higher, pulling with her arms. The vines were holding, at least for now, but she didn't know how long they'd last.

She made another foothold in the wall of the ravine, and then another. The muscles in her legs and arms quivered with exertion—and fear. Alex's life—both their lives—depended on her survival. She had to get to the top and signal Glenn when he flew over.

Gasping for breath, Dana pulled another few inches upward. Then she reached out with both hands and dug into the hard earth at the edge of the ravine. She'd made it, but she still had to get her body over. She gave one great lurch and managed to hook her upper arms onto the rim. It was excruciating, but she didn't give up, making a final all-out effort to heave her torso across the top.

Squirming like a snake, calling up every extra ounce of energy she possessed, she threw herself onto the dirt, dug in with elbows and knees until she was free of the vines and over the top. Then she rolled away from the edge and lay in the dirt only long enough to catch her breath before crawling back toward the abyss.

She couldn't see Alex, couldn't even see the ledge he'd fallen onto, if there was such a place. As far as she could tell, he'd vanished into the cool green of leaves and vines.

She was afraid he was dead.

Across the ravine, she saw the elephants, no more than forty feet away, milling wildly on the other side of the chasm and kicking up a cloud of dust with their huge deadly feet. They were so near, she could look into their crazed eyes, but they were no danger to her now.

Finally, like a sleepwalker, Dana got up and headed for the plateau. It was bare of trees, much like the clearing on the other side, another perfect landing spot for Glenn's plane. She shielded her eyes with her hands and searched the skies. The sun beat down, and in the glare she saw a hundred other suns reflected again and again. But no plane.

She dropped to the ground. There was no possibility of returning to the shade; she had to stay here, in the open, so Glenn could see her. She would wait as long as necessary.

It seemed like hours before she heard something, the faint hum of a motor. She got up, planted herself in the center of the open plateau and began to wave her arms and shout at the plane that appeared out of the blue sky.

"I'm here. Please land! Oh, please. Alex needs help!"

She knew that Glenn couldn't hear her, but she needed to say the words and let him at least see her desperation.

He flew over the mission, where the rendezvous with Alex was planned. The plane was so low that the trees swayed with the breeze it created before Glenn headed in the direction of the forest. The elephants, frightened by the sound, ran frantically back and forth along the ravine.

Just before hitting the tops of the trees, Glenn shot upward, looped and disappeared, leaving Dana hopelessly waving her arms at the little dot in the sky.

Then, suddenly, he was back, making another sweep of the area, flying even lower, dipping toward the chasm. She could see him clearly now. Their eyes met, he smiled and held a thumb upward.

They were saved!

"WELL, that's the damnedest thing I've ever heard. Alex Jourdan actually jumped off the bridge to save your life? Doesn't sound like the Alex I know. That one never had a hero complex.'' Glenn smiled broadly, revealing white, even teeth that looked even brighter against skin burned deep brown by the African sun.

Very quickly, Dana realized that the soft-spoken Glenn Bedell didn't mince his few words. He was obviously one of those men who'd been everywhere and done everything and didn't need to talk about his exploits. They showed in his deeply creased face and his snow-white hair, which was covered by a broad-brimmed hat. A cowboy of the African jungle, as he spoke he coiled a rope in his hand and surveyed the ravine.

''This where he jumped?''

''Yes, right below here,'' Dana replied.

Glenn walked along the chasm, gazing down intently, not commenting. Then he stopped and moved closer to the edge. His trained eyes had spotted something. ''There he is.''

Dana looked down, seeing only thick green vegetation. ''I don't see him. Where?'' she asked frantically.

''Move closer and look to the left of that spiky shrub. See, right there.'' He directed her gaze. ''You can glimpse his trouser leg.''

Dana saw him, and her heart skipped a beat.

''Trouble is, I don't see any sign of movement,'' Glenn told her. ''That concerns me.''

His remark ended Dana's momentary surge of euphoria. ''He may just be knocked out,'' she said hopefully.

''Well, let's find out. I can rig a rope on one of the trees and get down there to him. Problem is, I need someone up here with the strength to get us back.''

He looked Dana up and down. She could imagine how she appeared to him. Thin and haggard, wild-eyed and hysterical, not someone to depend on in any emergency. She tried to slow her breathing, calm her voice. "I'm going down there."

Not the type to argue, Glenn asked just one question. "Are you sure you can make it?"

"I've climbed mountains back home, and I know how to rappel down. Once I get there, you have the strength—and the know-how—to pull us out."

Glenn nodded. "I can get you out. If you can make it."

Her answer was to take the rope and loop it around herself, fashioning a makeshift harness. She was calm now and sure of her purpose. "I can make it. I have to find out if he's hurt or—" She bit back the hated words, not allowing herself to think that Alex might be dead.

Glenn nodded understandingly. "Take it slow going down and give me a pull on the rope when you hit the ledge. I'll bring Alex up first and then you." He raised a bushy gray eyebrow. "Are you sure you're up to this?"

Dana checked the ropes around her waist and across her chest. "Let me tell you just how sure I am, Glenn. I recently broke out of a Congolese jail. I've lived among the Pygmies, been attacked by hippos, escaped from an elephant stampede and a machine-gun attack. I lassoed Alex and pulled him out of quicksand, so you might say I'm good with ropes. By the way, I've even killed a man. Right now, there's nothing I can't face. So please lower me to the ledge. Alex needs me."

As she listed her recent encounters, the look on the bush pilot's face registered stunned disbelief. Without another word, he wrapped the end of the rope around a tree and, bracing his feet, began to lower Dana down the side of the cliff.

DANA'S FEET touched the ledge. She pushed against it, giving herself room to maneuver, then came to rest solidly beside Alex's motionless body. As she knelt beside him, she saw that his face was deathly white. Praying silently, she fell across his body, holding him close, listening for a heartbeat.

She heard it immediately, strong and even. He was alive!

From above she felt a tug on the rope.

"Sorry," she called up, tugging in return. "I forgot."

"Is he alive?"

"Yes, but he's unconscious," Dana yelled.

"Take it slow and check him out. We've got time."

Dana had no idea what to do first. She knew that if Alex's back or neck was broken, moving him could be fatal. But how was she supposed to check him out?

There was barely enough room on the ledge for her to kneel beside him, but she did the one thing that came naturally. She dabbed with the tail end of her shirt at the blood that oozed from a cut near his hairline. And she talked to him.

"Please wake up, Alex. Please be all right. I couldn't bear it if anything happened to you." She smoothed his hair and fought the prickle of tears in her eyes. "I'm supposed to check you out, but I don't even know how. You have to tell me what's the matter, Alex."

His chest rose and fell gently, but otherwise there was no movement. His eyes didn't open.

"You're such a fool," she chided, trying another tack. "Acting the hero. The role doesn't fit you, according to Glenn. But I know you did it to save me."

She leaned over and put her cheek next to his. His body was warm; his beard tickled her face. But he didn't move. The tears began to flow from her eyes, down her face, onto his unshaven chin. She kept on talking, saying everything that was in her heart.

"I tried to pretend that I didn't like you when we first met, but I was just afraid of my feelings, scared of letting go. You were dangerous, and that intrigued me, excited me—and terrified me at the same time."

She felt Alex stir, and she sat up, waiting for something to happen. From above, Glenn urged her to get moving, at least give him a report.

She ignored him and kept on talking to Alex. "We've been through so much together." His shirt was torn open, and she touched his bare chest, which was scratched and bruised from the fall. "These past days have seemed like a lifetime. A lifetime that we've shared, you and I. We've shared everything, Alex." She moved her hand along his warm, damp chest. He felt very much alive to her, very vital. If only he would open his eyes, speak to her.

"I love you, Alex. I can't lose you now. Promise me you'll be all right. Promise me you won't die." She leaned over and rested her head on his chest, just below his heart, listening to it beat, listening to the sound of life. "Promise me," she whispered desperately.

At first she wasn't even aware that his arms were around her; it seemed so natural, so right. Then she realized that he'd moved. He was hugging her!

"I'll promise you anything as long as you give me a kiss, Dana," he said in a barely audible voice.

"Alex!"

Without waiting for an answer, he kissed her—long and hard, as if savoring the taste of her. She returned the kiss and then broke away and sat up, looking into his laughing green eyes.

"You rat," she said. "You were awake all along, listening to me pour my heart out!"

Alex pushed himself to one elbow and looked into her eyes. "I swear, I was out until you promised me anything. That's enough to wake a man up. Now, about that promise..."

"Later," she answered shakily. "Right now, all that matters is that you're okay. *Are* you okay?" she added.

"I think so."

"Can you move?"

Alex flexed his legs and arms and pulled himself to a sitting position. "Battered, bruised but basically in good shape." He cocked an eyebrow and looked at Dana, encased in her rope harness. "Thanks to you."

She smiled in relief. He was all right!

"My God, woman, you are amazing." He stroked her arm thoughtfully. "How many rescues does this make, anyway?"

Dana laughed. "Who's counting?"

"Well, I am. And I can always count on you."

She touched his cheek with her fingertips. "At least for a while. Until we reach Nairobi."

"Ah. Nairobi. Hot showers and soft beds." He leaned forward and kissed her again. "And a date with my favorite heroine, the unstoppable Dana Baldwin."

He was about to steal another kiss when a voice boomed toward them from above. "Hello, down there! Let's get this show on the road."

Chapter Twelve

Hotel Inter-Continental
Nairobi, Kenya

How seductive civilization was, Dana mused, with all its comforts and conveniences. Within hours of her arrival in Nairobi, she was wrapped in its pleasurable folds, sitting in an air-conditioned room in a luxury hotel, sipping a cold soft drink, wearing a new robe and talking long distance to her brother Kurt.

"My contact at the embassy said my passport was in the works. I'll have it tomorrow," she told him.

"So you mentioned my partner's name," Kurt said with a laugh that was strong and clear over the phone lines.

"Of course. The fact that he's a friend of the ambassador's son didn't hurt at all!"

"What about the money Andy wired? He was pretty worried about you stuck there with no cash."

Dana took a long sip of her iced drink before answering. "The money's in my purse. There's a bank right next to the hotel, so it wasn't a problem. And a new credit card is being express mailed. I'm going to be a real person again."

"Good," her brother said. "Now, let's hear more about how you got in this mess, Sis. I can't get the story straight. Why were you wandering around in the middle of a rain forest alone?"

Dana swung her feet to the floor and stood up. "How I got separated from my tour is a long story, too long to go into now. I'll put it all together when I see you." Dana paced the carpeted floor. What she'd told her brother so far wasn't really a lie—that she'd wandered alone across the border into Zaire and then found her way into Kenya. It was just a slight whitewashing of the truth. "The whole story's—well, it's complicated," she added."

"Complicated is right, and Andy and I want to hear every adventurous detail. And we want you back home where we can keep our eyes on you. We miss you, Dana."

"I miss you, too. I have a lot to tell you." Suddenly she was anxious to get off the phone and keep any more questions from Kurt at bay awhile longer. Her tale had holes in it that wouldn't take much longer for his lawyer's brain to focus on like a laser beam.

"We're looking forward to seeing you. Love you, Sis."

Dana felt a glaze of tears across her eyes. "I love you, too, Kurt, and I'll see you soon. Thanks for everything."

She hung up the phone, thinking how lucky she was to have Kurt and Andy on her side—and Glenn, who'd gotten her safely to the American Embassy. Her luck held when the embassy accepted, with very few questions, her story of being a lone, lost tourist. And it was still holding. Not a word about her problems with the law in Porte Ivoire had reached the outside world.

Glenn had offered to alert the officials in Zaire about the deaths of Millicent and Yassif and the destruction of the Congo Waterways helicopter. Soon she'd write to Kantana and tell him the identity of the real murderer, but until she had her passport in hand and was safely out of Kenya, Dana had no intention of revealing her association with Congo Waterways Tours, Porte Ivoire, Louis Bertrand and certainly not the theft of the Elephant d'Or.

Dana turned up the air-conditioning and padded across the thick carpet to her bed. Her new purchases were spread out on it, a silky white dress for tonight with lacy underwear and all the accessories, a pantsuit for traveling, even a canvas bag to pack her purchases in for the final leg of her trip—the return flight to Tangiers, where her adventure had begun.

Alex was due at seven o'clock. She hadn't seen him since he'd dropped her off at the embassy, where she'd followed his advice and not mentioned his name to the officials. "Let's just say that my reputation may have preceded me," he explained to her with a shrug.

So she'd edited Alex from the story she told the officials at the embassy. That didn't mean he was out of her thoughts; far from it. Even when her situation was still unsettled, she'd thought of nothing except Alex. But she didn't see him, or even talk to him, for a day and a half. She had no way to get in touch with him. For her own sake, Alex said, he wouldn't reveal his whereabouts. He would come to her.

While she had no idea where he was, Dana had her suspicions about what he was doing—putting out feelers to sell the elephant.

When he finally called, it was with plans for their farewell dinner. She was eager to see him but didn't mention their rescue or her spontaneous declarations of love in the ravine. As she got dressed for their date, Dana promised herself she wouldn't mention the episode if he didn't. And she knew he wouldn't. After all, it had been a wild and crazy thing. But the truth was, she'd meant every word. She could never admit that to him; she had trouble admitting it even to herself.

Dana slipped off her robe and thoughtfully pulled on her panties and bra. She wasn't sorry, she decided, about telling Alex she loved him. But it didn't matter anyway because after tonight they'd never see each other again.

ALEX ARRIVED on time, carrying a bouquet of flowers. That surprised her, but no more than the gaily wrapped package he presented next. She held it gingerly in her hand as he kissed her on the cheek.

"You look beautiful," he told her. "No one would guess you'd been to hell and back."

Dana felt shy as she stood there holding the flowers in one hand and the present in the other. It seemed strange to be having a first date with a man she'd slept with so many nights. And once made love to.

She put the gift on the bedside table but still held on to the flowers. "You look—beautiful, too," she blurted out.

He was wearing beige trousers of a rough linen weave and a dark blue silk shirt. He looked thinner and tougher but just as handsome—and just as dangerous—as the first time she'd seen him.

He brushed his chin with a casual stroke of his hand. "Nice to have the beard off. I feel more like my old self."

There was an awkward silence, which Dana finally broke. "I'll put the flowers in water." She filled a pitcher and carefully arranged the flowers in it. "Thank you, Alex."

"I wanted to do something special for our last night together in Nairobi."

Dana blinked back tears. The last-night remark verified her feelings of what was to come. But she vowed not to get all maudlin and weepy about it.

She kept her voice steady and upbeat as she asked, "Have you thought any more about the plot against us? I mean Yassif and Millie, their determination to track us down and get the elephant."

"I haven't given it a moment's thought," Alex said, placing two fingers gently on her lips. "And I don't believe we should spend any of our time together discussing it."

Dana sank into the soft cushions of the sofa. "I feel guilty about it, though, Alex."

"For God's sake, why?

"I saw Millie and Yassif talking together more than once on the *Congo Queen*. I thought it was all very innocent, but I should have realized that something was going on."

"Would you have figured out the truth—that those two were planning to go after the prize?"

"No, of course not."

"Then don't worry about it. They were plotting thieves. And Millicent was a murderer."

"I wonder if Millie wasn't a little in love with Yassif—"

"The man made his living off women."

"Yes, but love can do strange things to people," Dana mused. Thinking of herself, she felt a blush rise to her cheeks and looked away quickly. "It's still difficult to imagine her going off the deep end about Yassif."

"It was the elephant, Dana."

"Yes, that damned elephant."

"She wanted it, and so did Yassif. They needed each other, her brain, his brawn."

"Did you hear what she told me at the mission? That she spied on Louis and saw him steal the elephant? I wonder if she was suspicious of Louis before the party? Or was it simply chance that she saw him?"

Alex shrugged. "We'll never know. God, what a chain reaction the elephant set off. Millie followed Louis, hooked Yassif into the plot and they came after us—"

"And the Egyptian hired Longongo, who hired Mac to lead him through the jungle," Dana finished.

"Longongo." Alex laughed softly. "He's probably still out there wandering around, looking for Mac and the elephant. And worrying that someday he has to face the Egyptian with empty hands. That's more than he bargained for, I'll guarantee." Alex sat down beside her. "Of course, I got more than I bargained for, too."

"More than the elephant?" she asked.

"I'm not thinking about the damned elephant now Dana. I thinking about my other prize, my partner." He kissed her lightly. "Whom I'm going to miss." He kissed her again, a little more seriously. "Very much."

With a little sigh she returned his kiss. "I don't want to think about leaving."

"Then don't."

His next kiss was much more familiar, warm, hungry. His tongue found hers, and their breaths mingled. Dana closed her eyes and opened herself to him. She knew that what was happening between them was inevitable. She also knew it would make leaving him much more difficult.

But that would be later. Now she could only think of being in his arms. It seemed to Dana exactly where she belonged.

"Your new dress is very pretty," he said. "Too bad."

She looked up at him, puzzled.

"Because I'm going to strip it off of you right now, and we're going to make love like never before."

"Right here?" she asked teasingly.

"Oh, no. In bed, a real bed this time," he murmured after another kiss. "And there'll be another difference, too. We'll be chasing no one. No one will be going after us. We'll take our time, slowly," he said with another kiss. "All night long until . . ."

"Until my plane leaves for Tangiers."

"Don't think about that now. It's a long time away."

THE BED was soft and wide, the sheets cool against their naked bodies. But their coolness didn't lower the temperature of her hot, fevered skin. It burned with need for him. And his lips were like a flame, igniting her wherever they touched, beginning with her breasts.

Dana moaned with pleasure as he sucked hungrily on her swollen nipple. And when he bit down, nibbling with his teeth, she felt a shimmer of heat cascade across her damp, flushed skin. Moving upward, he left a trail of hot kisses along her collarbone, her neck, her chin.

And then she came to life, reaching for him, kissing him long and hard. She held him tightly in her arms and rubbed her breasts sensuously against his hard chest, moved her hips and pelvis rhythmically, closer and closer, until she felt the hardness of him against her abdomen.

After that, the wave of anticipation that overcame her made Dana forget what the future held for her and Alex, forget their past problems, forget everything except the moment.

It was a passion-filled moment that freed her to give of herself completely, doing things she'd never thought to do before, never even imagined. She sucked and nibbled just as he'd done, first his mouth, then his earlobe, his flat brown nipple that responded to her teeth and tongue, hardening at her touch. And all the while her fingers stroked the shaft of his manhood. She looked at him, her chin resting on his chest, and watched through narrowed eyes the look of ecstasy that lit his face.

He closed his eyes and smiled. "I'm in heaven, Dana. Please don't stop."

"I've only just begun," she whispered, following her words with actions as she moved her lips downward to his abdomen, tasting his salty skin, and farther, to the hard line of his hipbone.

Alex moaned in pleasure, and Dana's heart almost exploded with joy at the sound. "Oh, God, Dana, I need you so much," he cried.

"And I need you, Alex."

That was enough for him. Almost roughly, he reached down and pulled her up and over the length of his body until her face was next to his. He cupped her chin gently in his hand and looked at her, his eyes hot with passion.

They turned over slowly, languidly, until he was on top and they were joined. As he entered her welcoming warmth, a tremor of desire pulsed through Alex that was as exciting as it was unexpected. He thought he knew what it would be like when they were together again, but this was more than he dreamed.

He lost control. Desire took over, shutting out the past, the future, time and place. Everywhere but here, everyone but Dana. He moved with her, breathed with her. Their hearts beat in rhythm. He was part of her and she of him. They were one.

DANA LAY CURLED in the warmth of Alex's body.

"I don't want to say goodbye," she told him in a whisper.

"Neither do I." He stroked her damp hair lovingly. "But you have a job, a life in Colorado. Not to mention two brothers who would beat the hell out of me if they knew what we'd been doing. Besides, I have a hot elephant on my hands."

Dana frowned. She didn't want to talk about the elephant but there was no way to avoid the subject. It dominated their lives.

"And the Egyptian has long arms," she said. "I remember."

"Yes. He's going to make it tough for me to dispose of the prize. And getting out of Kenya won't be easy, either, since I'm not a favorite of the customs officers, but I'll find a way."

She moved slightly, and he adjusted his body so that she fit into it perfectly.

"You wouldn't have those problems if you'd give it back, Alex."

"Give the elephant back? Never."

"I should have known better than to offer advice."

"Dana," he said, holding her closer. "Any advice from you is welcomed. But the elephant is a thing apart. You know that."

She nodded wordlessly.

"So let the elephant be. He's mine, and I'll do with him as I wish. Just as you'll do whatever you wish about your possessions in spite of my advice."

"What possessions?" she asked.

"Your notes, your tapes. When you write your book about the Pygmies, I hope that you'll do it for yourself. Not for your father. That's my advice."

"It's advice I'll take, Alex," she said. "Thank you."

"You deserve more, Dana. You're an incredible woman, and there's nothing you can't do. I've never known— Hell, you know how I feel."

Dana looked at him, smoothed his dark hair and kissed his forehead. "Tell me. Say it, Alex," she whispered. "I have my tickets. I'm on that plane tomorrow. So tell me what you feel. You don't have to be afraid."

"All right, I'll tell you what I feel." He took her hand and held it tightly. His eyes met hers squarely. "I love you, Dana."

She felt her heart lurch, but she didn't say anything, not yet.

"I've never said that to any other woman. You've been my partner, a thorn in my side, my perfect lover, my savior, my conscience. I've never shared with any other woman what I've shared with you."

He pulled her up onto his chest where she settled comfortably. "You know everything about me, and you still love me. Do you know how special that makes me feel?"

"And I've never been as close to anyone," she told him. "But we still have problems, Alex. We disagree about the elephant, and we live on opposite sides of the world."

"You're the one who told me that long-distance relationships don't work."

"I know. It's true, even though I hate to admit it." Cuddling close, Dana realized how much she would miss him—and the sense of adventure he'd given her. "When I met you, I was a law-abiding, conservative professor," Dana reminded him. "You turned me into a daredevil adventuress who has broken laws in three countries without a twinge of conscience."

"Now, Dana—"

"Well, maybe a twinge, but it wasn't heeded. Not when you were there to give me a secret life."

"That secret part of you was always there, Dana. I just unleashed it . . . for a while." He kissed her gently. "The law-abiding Dana is still inside of you. And I love and respect her, too."

"The law-abiding Dana wishes the Elephant d'Or didn't exist," she blurted.

"But it does, my love. I know you can't live under the shadow of illegality."

"No, Alex, I can't. It's not right, and nothing will ever make it right."

Alex nodded. "That's where we disagree, Dana. It's the difference between us. I could never live in your world. Middle-class morality doesn't fit my life-style."

"I know," she said softly.

"But we have the rest of tonight." He touched her cheek and let his fingers drift along her arm. "Later, we'll have that dinner I promised—in bed—and then breakfast—in bed. And between meals, I have a feeling you want what I want.''

Dana kissed his hand. ''I do. There's no doubt about it. For tonight at least,'' she said, ''I'm yours.''

''Then if you're mine, open my present.''

''Oh, I forgot.'' She reached for the package on the bedside table.

Alex urged her on. ''But hurry. I have an even better surprise waiting for you under the covers.''

Dana grinned impishly and tore off the wrappings.

Alex put his hands behind his neck, leaned back against the headboard and watched her. The soft light from the bathroom bathed her nakedness in a golden sheen. Simply looking at her gave him a thrill of pleasure. She was like a child tearing off the ribbons, tossing the papers on the floor. She'd be gone in less than twenty-four hours. Alex had adjusted to that fact, or thought he had. But suddenly losing her was more painful than he'd imagined.

''No, I don't believe it—an elephant,'' she said, falling in laughter against his chest. She held up a statue carved from teak and decorated with bits of silk cloth and pieces of shiny red, blue and green glass.

''I thought maybe you'd put it by your bed and think of me now and then. And what better symbol?''

Dana ran her fingers along the smooth wood of the teak figurine. ''The damned elephant,'' she said with a laugh, ''I'll never get away from it. And when I look at it, believe me, I'll think of you!'' She put the statue on the bedside table and kissed Alex. ''I'll never see life the same again.''

''I hope not,'' he said softly, kissing her neck.

''From now on, life will always be more vivid and alive and filled with excitement. I'll never take anything for granted, and if I have to break the rules now and then, I won't be afraid. You've given me that," she said, "and because of it, I think I can handle anything now."

Alex felt that funny little spasm near his heart again. He pulled Dana to him and held her tightly. His body cried out for her, and so did his heart. "I want to make love to you again, Dana," he whispered.

His kiss was filled with desperate longing, which she responded to completely. "And pretend," she whispered.

"Yes, pretend that we'll never have to say goodbye."

Epilogue

Institut de Langue
Tangiers, Morocco

Moving languidly in the afternoon heat, Dana put the last of her clothes into her suitcase. The summer session at the institute was officially over. Tomorrow she'd catch the plane back to Colorado, her family, her job.

She didn't want to go.

Dana sank down onto the bed and stared into space. She wasn't sure what she wanted to do, but her old life held no appeal, not after the excitement of her adventure with Alex. She wanted more of that. She wanted him.

But he was a criminal. Her background, her upbringing, her sense of morality told her she was right in leaving him. Two such diverse life-styles could never meld, not unless one of them gave in. Could she be the one? Could she forgive, even forget Alex's involvement in the elephant episode? She leaned back on the pillows, her mind whirling. Maybe he was right. If the elephant had no real owner, it belonged to the man who had it at the moment.

A shadow blocked the sunlight streaming through the open door. Dana looked up, startled, and then surged off the bed in one fluid movement.

"Alex! Oh, Alex."

She flung herself at him, not really believing he was there until she felt his arms around her, his lips on hers. Dana knew then she wanted him, no matter what he'd done in the past, no matter what he might do in the future.

"What—" she managed between kisses "—what are you doing here?"

"I've come to find you. What else?" He hugged her close.

"That's good," she said, "because I've been waiting for you—all my life." Dana laughed with sheer happiness, thinking how far they'd come since that first day in Porte Ivoire. She stepped back from his arms, her hand touching his face, still not really believing he was there. "How did you get out of Nairobi with the elephant?"

He grinned, the cocky smile she remembered—and loved—so well. "No problem," he said. "Because I didn't have the elephant."

"You sold it?"

He strode to her bedside table and picked up the teak statue he'd given her in Nairobi. "Has this little fellow made you think of me?" He ran his hand over the polished surface.

"I didn't need him for that. I've been thinking of you all the time, every minute of the day. But what about the Elephant d'Or?"

With another grin, he cracked the statue against the edge of the table. Its husk fell in pieces to the floor. "Well, well, look at that."

Dana gave a gasp as she saw what he held in his hand, a golden, jewel-encrusted treasure. "The Elephant d'Or," she said. "Inside *my* elephant!" Suddenly the impact of what he'd done hit her like a lightning bolt, and her joy erupted into rage.

"You rat! You used me to smuggle it into Tangiers! You used me again!" Dana swung out at him, flailing wildly. Filled with anger and self-disgust, she regretted every minute she'd spent in his lying arms.

Alex tried to protect himself from her attack and reason with her at the same time. "Stop for a minute. Just listen!" He grabbed her shoulders and guided her toward the bed where she fell back with him on top. Suddenly Alex started laughing.

Dana saw red. "Don't you dare laugh! This isn't funny."

"But it's getting to be a habit. In order to make you listen, I have to fall on you!"

Dana's response was to start struggling again, but he pinned her down easily. "Now," he said, "we can talk like civilized people."

"Civilized?" she snapped. "You? Never!"

Despite her struggles, he managed to kiss her. Dana turned her face away. "Not this time, Alex. I won't give in."

"But you will, Dana, when you hear my plan."

"I don't want to hear it, I don't want—"

He raised his voice, drowning out her protests. "I'm donating the elephant to a museum."

Dana quit struggling and lay absolutely still, immobilized by surprise. Finally, she found her voice. "You're doing what?"

"Donating it to a museum. I'll need your help in working out the details."